TURNING POINTS

By Meghan Green

THE HARLEM RENAISSANCE

Cavendish Square

New York

Published in 2021 by Cavendish Square Publishing, LLC
243 5th Avenue, Suite 136, New York, NY 10016

Website: cavendishsq.com

This publication represents the opinions and views of the author based on his or her personal experience, knowledge, and research. The information in this book serves as a general guide only. The author and publisher have used their best efforts in preparing this book and disclaim liability rising directly or indirectly from the use and application of this book.

Portions of this work were originally authored by Stuart A. Kallen and published as *The Harlem Renaissance* (*American History*). All new material this edition authored by Meghan Green.

All websites were available and accurate when this book was sent to press.

Cataloging-in-Publication Data

Names: Green, Meghan.
Title: The Harlem Renaissance / Meghan Green.
Description: New York : Cavendish Square, 2021. | Series: Turning points | Includes index.
Identifiers: ISBN 9781502657688 (pbk.) | ISBN 9781502657695 (library bound) | ISBN 9781502657701 (ebook)
Subjects: LCSH: Harlem Renaissance–Juvenile literature. | African Americans–Intellectual life–20th century–Juvenile literature. | African Americans–History–1877-1964–Juvenile literature. | African American intellectuals–New York (State)–New York–History–20th century–Juvenile literature. | African American arts–20th century–Juvenile literature. | Harlem (New York, N.Y.)–Intellectual life–20th century–Juvenile literature.
Classification: LCC E185.89.I56 G72 2021 | DDC 810.9'896073–dc23

Editor: Jennifer Lombardo
Copy Editor: Michelle Denton
Designer: Deanna Paternostro

Some of the images in this book illustrate individuals who are models. The depictions do not imply actual situations or events.

CPSIA compliance information: Batch #CS20CSQ: For further information contact Cavendish Square Publishing LLC, New York, New York at 1-877-980-4450.

Printed in China

Find us on

TABLE OF CONTENTS

THE REVIVAL
OF A CULTURE

The word "renaissance" means revival or rebirth. It's most frequently used to describe the revival of art and literature that occurred in Europe between the 14th and 16th centuries, but other groups have also experienced their own cultural renaissance. For many black Americans, a renaissance began in the 1920s. Harlem, a neighborhood in New York City, was the focal point; between 1918 and the mid-1930s, the neighborhood thrived as a centerpiece for black American culture and the movement known as the Harlem Renaissance.

The movement was primarily led by black writers, actors, singers, artists, and jazz and blues musicians. They came from many backgrounds and did not necessarily share the same beliefs about art, politics, or society. However, they all shared a common goal: They wanted to provide a voice for the 10 million black Americans trying to coexist with the 80 million white people living in the United States.

Working Toward Equality

The Harlem Renaissance lasted for about 12 years, beginning as World War I ended in 1918 and tapering off in the 1930s. However,

In the 1920s, Harlem (*shown here*) was a neighborhood of contradictions. Although it was a hotbed of cultural creativity, many of the residents were too poor to afford much of the entertainment that was available there.

the movement's impact lingered for several decades and, in fact, can still be felt today.

In large part, the Harlem Renaissance resulted from the ongoing struggle black Americans had with extreme poverty, racism, segregation, and institutional violence in nearly every American city and state. Under the government policy of segregation in many states and communities, black Americans were kept separate from white Americans. This prevented them from finding good jobs, buying homes, and attending decent schools. Black Americans were commonly prohibited from using public spaces, including swimming pools, parks, and restrooms. They patronized black-owned restaurants, theaters, clothing shops, and taverns instead.

Life was particularly difficult for black Americans living in the South and in rural areas of the Midwest. A hate group called the Ku Klux Klan (KKK) was a powerful social and political force in many states. Mayors, police chiefs, and even state legislators and governors were among its millions of members. The KKK terrorized black and immigrant communities. In addition, many black Americans were victims of lynching. Lynching means killing someone by mob action for an alleged crime. Since most people who were killed were completely innocent, black people lived in fear much of the time, never knowing when they might be targeted.

This violence, coupled with poor economic conditions and race riots in many cities, led many black southerners to uproot their lives. In what has been called the Great Migration, millions of African Americans moved to industrial cities in the North, such as New York City, where there was a greater degree of freedom and opportunity.

Paul Laurence Dunbar, whose parents had been slaves, achieved fame writing about life in the poetic dialect of southern African Americans. Dunbar's 1902 book, *The Sport of the Gods*, was the first novel about black life in New York City. In it, Dunbar described the mythical status the city held in the imaginations of black southerners:

> They had heard of New York as a place vague and far away, a city that, like Heaven, to them had existed by faith alone. All the

Members of the KKK struck terror into the hearts of black Americans, who knew they could be targeted at any time even if they had done nothing wrong. Because of the group's strong hold on the South, many black people moved to the North.

days of their lives they had heard about it, and it seemed to them the centre of all the glory, all the wealth, and all the freedom of the world.[1]

Like some European immigrants, who had heard rumors that New York's streets were paved with gold, the reality of the city may have disappointed some African Americans. Unskilled black women living in Harlem labored as maids, dressmakers, beauticians, and cooks. Men were hired as elevator operators, shoe shiners, porters, doormen, messengers, waiters, janitors, and day laborers. However, even these low-paying jobs presented better opportunities than those in the South. Additionally, unlike most of the South, Harlem had many black-owned shops and restaurants as well as opportunities for black professionals, including lawyers, doctors, nurses, teachers, and preachers.

Spreading Cultural Influence

While a few black business owners, landlords, and artists were financially successful, many Harlem residents remained poor before, during, and after the renaissance. However, the mix of old and new cultures—from the South, New York City, and foreign countries—provided artistic inspiration for those leading the Harlem Renaissance. As history professor Cary D. Wintz wrote in *Black Culture and the Harlem Renaissance*,

> *[The neighborhood] provided the material and the setting for many literary creations of the Renaissance. The poetry, short stories, and novels of the period abound with scenes and characters lifted from Harlem's streets and cabarets ... Harlem though ... was a teeming, overcrowded ghetto, and much of its laughter and gaiety only thinly veiled the misery and poverty that was becoming the standard of life for the new black urban masses. This, too, was reflected by the Harlem Renaissance.*[2]

What made the era so unique was the fact that more than just black people were celebrating black culture. This was one of the first times that black and white Americans read the same literature, attended theater productions together, danced together, and sang together. It was a brief period, and it did not mark the end of racism. However, for those in New York City's black communities, the renaissance proved to be a celebration of pride, culture, identity, and history. For the first time, the achievements of black Americans were visible for all to see—and after three centuries of injustice, enslavement, and prejudice, black Americans were given the attention they deserved.

INWOOD
HUDSON HEIGHTS
WASHINGTON HEIGHTS
SUGAR HILL
HAMILTON HEIGHTS
MANHATTAN-VILLE
MORNINGSIDE HEIGHTS
HARLEM
EAST HARLEM
UPPER WEST SIDE
MANHATTAN VALLEY
CENTRAL PARK
UPPER EAST SIDE
YORKVILLE
LINCOLN SQUARE
LENOX HILL
HELL'S KITCHEN
THEATER DISTRICT
MIDTOWN
SUTTON PLACE
MIDTOWN EAST
GARMENT DISTRICT
MURRAY HILL
KIPS BAY
CHELSEA
ROSE HILL
FLATIRON DISTRICT
GRAMERCY PARK
STUYVESANT TOWN
UNION SQUARE
WEST VILLAGE
GREENWICH VILLAGE
NOHO
BOWERY
EAST VILLAGE
ALPHABET CITY
SOHO
NOLITA
LOWER EAST SIDE
LITTLE ITALY
TRIBECA
CHINATOWN
TWO BRIDGES
CIVIC CENTER
BATTERY PARK CITY
FINANCIAL DISTRICT

CHAPTER ONE

CHANGE IN THE CITY

In the early 1900s, Harlem was home to more than 150,000 black people who represented a melting pot of American-born black citizens from around the United States as well as immigrants from Jamaica, Haiti, Cuba, and various African countries. In 1925, Harlem had only been the center of black urban culture for about 15 years. How it transformed into the "World's Greatest Negro Metropolis" can be traced to a combination of capitalism, poverty, opportunity, and racism.

Historian Leon Litwack described the early decades of the 20th century as "the most violent and repressive period in the history of race relations in the United States."[1] This was especially true in Virginia, Louisiana, Alabama, Mississippi, Georgia, and the Carolinas, where 80 percent of black Americans lived in rural areas as sharecroppers. Sharecropping was a system under which people—mainly black people—farmed land owned by others in exchange for a small percentage of the crops. Sharecroppers were the poorest of the poor, often working long hours, living in bad conditions, and suffering from malnutrition and ill health.

Between 1910 and 1930, about 1.5 million black southerners moved north to escape this lifestyle. In addition to New York,

Harlem is one of the many famous neighborhoods that make up the island of Manhattan in New York City. It can be seen on this modern-day map of Manhattan.

they settled in cities such as Chicago, Illinois; Detroit, Michigan; Cleveland, Ohio; and Philadelphia, Pennsylvania. The Great Migration, as it became known, completely changed the face of Manhattan. In six years, the black population of Harlem doubled from 50,000 to more than 100,000. One-quarter of the black population was from New York City, while another quarter came from foreign countries. The other half came from the South and the Midwest. Between 1902 and 1925, another 50,000 black Americans migrated to the city. By 1930, Harlem's black population had exceeded 200,000.

Philip A. Payton Jr.

Harlem's residents were almost entirely white in 1901, when two landlords who lived next to each other got into an argument. What started the disagreement is a mystery, but it ended up changing history. One landlord decided to anger his rival by hiring Philip A. Payton Jr. to fill his empty building with black tenants. Payton, a porter who desperately wanted to become the city's first black real estate agent, had no problem finding tenants—there was an extreme housing shortage for black people in Manhattan because few landlords would rent to them. Payton managed the property and convinced other landlords to let him manage their houses and apartments.

In 1903, Payton was so successful that he spent $500,000 (equal to approximately $14.7 million in 2018) to found the Afro-American Realty Company in downtown Manhattan. Within a few years, Payton was known as the "Father of Harlem," having changed the racial character of the neighborhood almost single-handedly. Payton's company failed a few years later, but by that time, other black real estate agents were following in his footsteps. Not only were black people moving into apartment buildings, they were also purchasing properties in the neighborhood.

Not everyone was happy with Harlem's black migration. White residents began fleeing in large numbers from what they called the "Negro invasion." Many white residents felt that having black neighbors lowered their social status and property value.

FROM THE SOURCE: "THE MAKING OF HARLEM"

Author, educator, and early civil rights activist James Weldon Johnson was one of the leading literary voices of the Harlem Renaissance. In Alain Locke's book *The New Negro*, Johnson described Harlem:

In the make-up of New York, Harlem is not merely a Negro colony or community, it is a city within a city, the greatest Negro city in the world. It is not a slum or a fringe, it is located in the heart of Manhattan and occupies one of the most beautiful and healthful sections of the city. It is not a "quarter" of dilapidated tenements, but is made up of [new] apartments and handsome dwellings, with well-paved and well-lighted streets. It has its own churches, social and civic centers, shops, theatres and other places of amusement. And it contains more Negroes to the square mile than any other spot on earth. A stranger who rides up magnificent Seventh Avenue on a bus or in an automobile must be struck with surprise at the transformation which takes place after he crosses One Hundred and Twenty-fifth Street. Beginning there, the population suddenly darkens and he rides through twenty-five solid blocks where the passers-by, the shoppers, those sitting in restaurants, coming out of theatres, standing in doorways and looking out of windows are practically all Negroes ... There is nothing just like it in any other city in the country, for there is no preparation for it; no change in the character of the houses and streets; no change, indeed, in the appearance of the people, except their color.[1]

1. James Weldon Johnson, "Harlem: The Culture Capital," in Alain Locke, ed., *The New Negro* (New York, NY: Touchstone, 1997), pp. 301–02.

Shown here is a row of tenements in Harlem.

The departure of the white residents opened up more opportunities for the black community, as people were able to purchase or rent the vacated properties. By 1911, black Americans had purchased 10 percent of Harlem's large apartment buildings, called tenements, and 40 percent of its private homes.

Economic Opportunities

The drop in real estate prices was only part of the way the economic picture was improving for many people living in Harlem. In 1914, World War I began in Europe. Even before the United States joined the fight and declared war on Germany in April 1917, the government was active in aiding its European allies. Industries were ordered to produce a record number of weapons, clothes, rations, and other wartime goods. At the same time, the war cut off the steady supply of white laborers who had been emigrating from Europe to New York since the 1880s. This created a labor shortage, and some employers began hiring black laborers. Black people kept leaving the rural South in ever-increasing numbers.

For the first time, black laborers were making good wages, saving money, and investing in real estate. By 1920, it was not unusual for a black family to walk into a real estate office and put down anywhere from $1,000 to $5,000 in cash to purchase property.

Some of the stories of black entrepreneurs making fortunes in real estate are legendary. In 1925, James Weldon Johnson wrote a story about Lillian Harris Dean, known as "Pig Foot Mary." She had become successful by selling "soul food," such as fried chicken and pickled pig's feet, from a small stand in Harlem. Johnson wrote:

> *"Pig Foot Mary" is a character in Harlem. Everybody who knows the corner of Lenox Avenue and One Hundred and Thirty-fifth Street knows "Mary" and her stand, and has been tempted by the smell of her pigsfeet, fried chicken and hot corn, even if he has not been a customer. "Mary" … bought the five-story apartment house at the corner of Seventh Avenue and One Hundred and Thirty-seventh Street at a price of $42,000. Later she sold it to the Y.W.C.A. for dormitory purposes … [for] $72,000.*[2]

Success stories of this type were common in the neighborhood. The total value of property owned by black Americans in Harlem in 1925 exceeded $60 million. The buying and selling created some of the first black real estate moguls in New York history. In 1925, Johnson wrote:

> *[This is] amazing, especially when we take into account the short time in which [it happened]. Twenty years ago Negroes were begging for the privilege of renting a flat in Harlem. Fifteen years ago, barely a half dozen colored men owned real property in all Manhattan. And down to ten years ago, the amount that had been acquired in Harlem was comparatively negligible. Today [1925] Negro Harlem is practically owned by Negroes.*[3]

The Start of a Movement

Now that they were no longer struggling simply to survive, many black people could afford to spend more time on creative activities that showcased their pride in their heritage and various cultures. Many historians believe the catalyst of the New Negro movement—a term often used in conjunction with the Harlem Renaissance—was a victory parade held on February 17, 1919, several months after the end of World War I. On that sunny winter morning, approximately 1,300 veterans from the all-black 369th Infantry Regiment, nicknamed the Harlem Hellfighters, marched along Fifth Avenue with their military jazz band, led by the legendary trumpeter Lieutenant James Reese Europe.

The white audiences downtown applauded politely for the black soldiers, but after they crossed over to Lenox and entered Harlem, they received a heroes' welcome. Girlfriends and relatives joined the ranks of soldiers, and a torrent of pennants, flags, banners, and scarves rained down on the men. According to the newspaper *New York Age*,

> *Never in the history of [New York] has such a rousing royal welcome been given returning heroes from the field of battle; not for many a day is it likely that thousands of white and colored citizens will participate in such a tumultuous and enthusiastic demonstration …*

> *In Harlem the greeting bordered on riot. Amid exciting scenes and the band playing "Here Comes My Daddy Now," the Hell Fighters marched between two howling walls of humanity from 125th to 140th Street. Those unable to secure standing room on the sidewalk [hung from windows and lampposts], while from the rooftops thousands stood and whooped things up.*[4]

Black veterans were among the most eager to fight for equal rights after the war. However, there was a political divide within the black American community. On one side, older black leaders such as William Edward Burghardt (W. E. B.) Du Bois, cofounder of the National Association for the Advancement of Colored

Shown here are the Harlem Hellfighters marching in their 1919 victory parade.

THEY MADE HISTORY:
THE HARLEM HELLFIGHTERS

The 369th Infantry Regiment was made up of the first black troops sent to fight on the European battlefront in World War I. They spent 191 continuous days engaged in trench warfare, and their bravery was legendary on both sides of the conflict: While the German enemy called them the "*Blutlustige Schwarze Männer,*" or "bloodthirsty black men," the French called them heroes. The 369th was the only American unit awarded the Croix de Guerre, the French High Command's highest mark of honor.

The Harlem Hellfighters were among 380,000 black Americans who served during World War I. These soldiers faced severe discrimination and segregation within the military. Also, after spending time in France, the black soldiers discovered they had more rights in Europe than they did in the United States. In 1919, Lieutenant William N. Colson wrote in a Chicago black newspaper called *Defender,*

> *While in France, the Negro soldiers ... discovered that the only white men that treated them as men were native Europeans, and especially the French with their wider social experience and finer social sense. The Frenchman was unable to comprehend American color prejudice. The Englishman was much more democratic than the American.*[1]

This fair treatment helped the heroes of Harlem return home with a new sense of dignity. They were done cowering under white racism and were willing to take risks to prove their worth to a society that had never valued their contributions.

1. Quoted in Theodore G. Vincent, ed., *Voices of a Black Nation* (Trenton, NJ: Africa World, 1990), p. 68.

People (NAACP), worked with white supporters and believed that nonviolence was the path to equality and integration. Some felt these efforts were geared toward helping only the small number of middle-class black Americans and professionals. This alienated young black radicals who called themselves "New Negroes" to distinguish themselves from traditional leaders. The New Negroes did not necessarily believe in integration. Many believed direct—and even violent—action was the only solution to their problems.

The New Negroes supported black nationalism and black liberation—movements that struck fear into the heart of the white establishment. Black nationalists believed black people should be proud of their heritage and advocated building separate communities based on black pride. Black war veterans, who were leading members of the New Negro movement, were ready to fight back against the KKK and others who were lynching black people on a regular basis in the South.

Establishing Black Independence

The indisputable leader of the New Negro movement was Marcus Garvey—not a war veteran or a southerner but an immigrant from Jamaica, a country with a strong African influence. The British had populated the island with African slaves after the native inhabitants were killed by colonial violence and the spread of infectious diseases, so most Jamaican people today have at least some African heritage.

Garvey moved to the United States in 1916. The following year, he established the headquarters of the Universal Negro Improvement Association (UNIA) in Harlem. The UNIA began with 13 members, including Garvey, but quickly grew beyond the borders of Harlem. Garvey believed in Pan-Africanism, which is the idea that all people of African descent, no matter where they live in the world, share a common heritage and should support each other. For this reason (among others), people sometimes refer to Africa as if it was a country rather than a continent made up of separate countries. It also incorporated the idea of independence, and people who subscribed to Pan-Africanism had been calling for European countries to end their

PAST MEETS PRESENT: FIGHTING FOR RECOGNITION

Although society has come a long way since World War I, racism still persists today, and many black people have difficulty getting the recognition they deserve. One example involves Corporal Waverly "Woody" Woodson Jr., a soldier who fought in the only black regiment to storm the beach at Normandy in World War II. Woodson was wounded in the battle but continued to fight, saving the lives of many fellow soldiers. Years later, he was nominated for the Medal of Honor for his bravery in combat. However, he never received it.

At the time, black people were routinely denied their hard-earned medals by the US Army. In 1997, President Bill Clinton "awarded the nation's highest award for valor in 1997 to seven black soldiers who'd been denied their D-Day decorations by an Army afflicted by institutional racism."[1] However, Woodson was not one of them. He died in 2005 and, as of 2020, his widow is still fighting to get his medal and have his contributions to the war effort recognized.

1. Linda Hervieux, "He Served With D-Day's Only African-American Combat Unit. His Widow Is Still Fighting for His Medal of Honor," *TIME*, modified June 4, 2019, time.com/5599905/d-day-barrage-balloon-hero.

colonization of African countries. Garvey took this idea a step further, calling for all black Americans to move to Africa, where he felt they would have more economic opportunities and would be given more respect. Garvey's philosophy is often called "Garveyism."

The idea that black people should separate themselves from white American society and move to Africa was not new. In 1816, an organization called the American Society for Colonizing the Free People of Color of the United States—often shortened to the American Colonization Society—was founded by influential white men and received some financial backing from the federal government.

The organization opposed the practice of slavery but also believed it would be impossible—and undesirable for people of all races—to integrate freed black slaves into white American society. For this reason, they bought land in Africa, founded the country of Liberia, and paid to send black people to live there. Garvey and the UNIA later tried to colonize Liberia to create a bond between that country and the United States, but their plan failed. However, it is important to note the difference between the American Colonization Society and Garveyism. Under Garveyism, black Americans were making

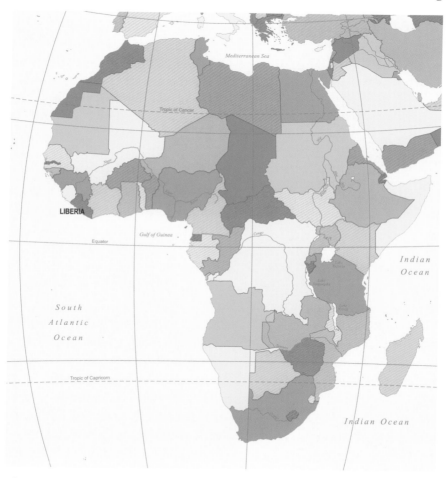

Liberia was established as a place for black people to move to after being freed from slavery. Some people embraced this idea; others rejected it.

the choice to separate themselves and move to Africa. Not everyone was required to support Garvey's vision, and in fact, not everyone did; some black people whose families had been living in the United States for decades rejected the idea that they should move to a continent they had never set foot on. In contrast, the American Colonization Society was making that choice for them and refusing to let them join white society.

Any person of African descent could join the UNIA for 35 cents and a pledge to support the association. Within months of its founding, the UNIA swelled to 12,000 members. By 1918, its influential newspaper had a circulation of 500,000. In 1920, Garvey claimed there were 3 million UNIA members in the United States, Central and South America, and the Caribbean. While some experts believe Garvey inflated the membership numbers, there is little doubt that the UNIA had a powerful influence in Harlem, where about one out of every three residents belonged to the organization.

Taking advantage of his widespread support, Garvey planned several money-making projects to pay for his dream of founding an independent black nation. He promoted black nationalism by providing employment and economic independence through several successful business ventures in Harlem. These businesses, which were staffed and run by black Americans, were financed through donations. Garvey's Negro Factories Corporation (NFC) established everything from laundries and restaurants to hotels, printers, and even a factory that specialized in making black dolls.

Within months, the NFC became a symbol of African American business expertise in Harlem. The company's businesses competed successfully with white-owned businesses, and the stores provided employment for Harlem residents who were denied jobs elsewhere. Hundreds of men and women found work as managers, clerks, accountants, stenographers, and secretaries. In addition, women were often put in positions of authority, which was considered quite unusual during an era when men dominated business and politics. The NFC invested in real estate, offices, and empty factories, and then rented them at a discount to faltering black-

Marcus Garvey and his views were controversial but influential during the Harlem Renaissance.

owned businesses. Garvey considered their success important to the black independence movement.

Nowhere was the New Negro movement more on display than the first UNIA convention, held in Harlem in August 1920. The event attracted 25,000 members. They named Garvey "His Excellency the Provisional President of Africa." In this role, he claimed to represent the governments of African nations and act as leader of all black people throughout the world. Garvey created his own Harlem royalty, bestowing titles such as Duke of the Nile and Viscount of Niger on his closest advisers. Bearers of these titles as well as Garvey himself appeared in military-style uniforms bedecked with medals and decorations, all tailor-made by the NFC. The UNIA also adopted a national flag—a red, black, and green banner said to represent the motherland, Africa.

After the opening ceremonies, the UNIA convention hosted a three-hour parade through Harlem that was grander than the one that welcomed the return of the Hellfighters. The uniformed Harlem royalty led 50,000 UNIA members in a procession that stretched 10 city blocks. Garvey was the central focus, seated in a Packard convertible and wearing a purple, green, and black uniform decorated with a gold braid and a hat with red plumes.

Criticism of Garveyism

Not all black Americans thought Garvey was a positive leader. The ceremony and public adulation concerned traditional black leaders who disagreed with Garvey's combination of politics and self-promotion. Du Bois was especially critical, noting that some had invested their entire life savings—unwisely, in Du Bois's view—in Garvey's various stock market offerings. In a 1921 article in *The Crisis*, the NAACP's magazine, Du Bois wrote that Garvey was "a stubborn, domineering leader of the mass; he has worthy industrial and commercial schemes but he is an inexperienced businessman. His ... methods are bombastic, wasteful, illogical and ineffective and almost illegal."[5]

Du Bois was not the only person examining the business practices of the UNIA. Garvey's Pan-African message frightened many within the US government who feared a violent black uprising. The Federal Bureau of Investigation (FBI), the State Department, military intelligence agents, and even the US Postal Service used the threat as an excuse to spy on Garvey. Postmaster General Roger Bowen stated that Garvey planned "to instill into the minds of negroes … that they have been greatly wronged and oppressed by the white races and that they can only hope for relief and redress through concerted and aggressive action on their part."[6]

In 1922, Garvey was formally charged with using the US Postal Service to defraud buyers of UNIA stock. He was convicted and imprisoned in a federal penitentiary in Atlanta, Georgia. In 1925, President Calvin Coolidge shortened his sentence, and Garvey was released in 1927 and deported to Jamaica, where many people still thought of him as a hero and freedom fighter.

Garvey spent much of the Harlem Renaissance fighting what some saw as prejudicial persecution by the US government. After Garvey went to jail, his wife, Amy Jacques Garvey, kept the UNIA alive, and the group's philosophies provided a strong political foundation for the Harlem Renaissance. By promoting racial consciousness and a powerful sense of independence and black pride, Garvey's philosophies provided hope in a time of despair. In part, Garvey's messages of pride helped inspire the writers, artists, and musicians who would become the faces of the Harlem Renaissance.

How You See History

1. Why do you think it was so important to black people to own property?

2. How did the victory parade for the Harlem Hellfighters inspire the New Negro movement?

3. Why was Garveyism controversial?

CHAPTER TWO

LITERATURE

The Harlem Renaissance affected many different cultural areas, including music, art, and theater. However, the intellectual basis for the entire movement came from the writers. These men and women were the leaders of what became known as Harlem's "Talented Tenth"—the 10 percent of the neighborhood residents who were successful doctors, lawyers, publishers, musicians, actors, and authors. The writers of the Harlem Renaissance were aware that the world was reading their works. They wanted to use that attention to increase public interest in black history and culture as well as to promote racial pride.

The promoters of the Harlem Renaissance were inspired by a previous generation that had written about their African heritage and black American folk culture in the late 1890s. For example, the American Negro Academy (ANA), founded in Washington, DC, in 1897, brought together black intellectuals who promoted black literature, arts, music, and history.

As an outgrowth of the ANA and its work, by the 1910s, there were at least 500 newspapers and magazines in the United States devoted to black social, historical, and cultural issues. In 1915, Carter G. Woodson, a Harvard PhD, cofounded the Association for the Study of Negro Life and History—the first black historical associa-

◀ Carter G. Woodson was the cofounder of the first black historical association, which published writing that highlighted black history.

FROM THE SOURCE: THE SOULS OF BLACK FOLK

The Souls of Black Folk, written by W. E. B. Du Bois, was extremely influential among the writers of the Harlem Renaissance. In the excerpt below, Du Bois examined the experience of being both black and American:

The history of the American Negro is the history of this strife, —this longing to attain self-conscious manhood, to merge his double self into a better and truer self. In this merging he wishes neither of the older selves to be lost. He would not Africanize America, for America has too much to teach the world and Africa. He would not bleach his Negro soul in a flood of white Americanism, for he knows that Negro blood has a message for the world. He simply wishes to make it possible for a man to be both a Negro and an American, without being cursed and spit upon by his fellows, without having the doors of Opportunity closed roughly in his face.[1]

1. W. E. B. Du Bois, *The Souls of Black Folk* (Chicago, IL: A. C. McClurg & Company, 1903), p. 4.

tion. This organization still publishes the *Journal of African American History* (originally named the *Journal of Negro History*) and was the first to promote Negro History Week, which later grew into Black History Month. This event is still recognized throughout North America each February and in October in Europe.

Feeling Conflicted

W. E. B. Du Bois was among the scholars who wrote papers for the ANA in its early years, and his 1903 book, *The Souls of Black Folk*, was groundbreaking. In the book, Du Bois put forth the idea that African Americans are torn between two conflicting worlds—their African heritage and their American homeland.

This idea resonated with many black people. For example, Harlem Renaissance writers Langston Hughes and James Weldon Johnson both credited *The Souls of Black Folk* for inspiring them in their early years. Hughes said it was "my earliest memory of any book ... except a schoolbook,"[1] while Johnson said it was "a work which ... has had a greater effect upon and within the Negro race in America than any other single [book] published."[2]

When poet Claude McKay read the book in 1912, he felt the same way. Born in Jamaica, McKay, too, felt that he was torn between his African roots and the traditions of the white colonists who governed his homeland. Living in Harlem in 1919, McKay was among the first poets to encapsulate the experiences of the black urban masses. He wrote "If We Must Die" during a period known as the Red Summer of 1919, when more than 30 race riots occurred in major American cities, including Charleston, South Carolina; Washington, DC; and Chicago, Illinois. The riots were largely attacks on black neighborhoods by unemployed white Americans who were angry that many factories had employed black laborers. During the Red Summer, 43 black men were lynched, 8 were burned at the stake, and hundreds died from other racial violence.

In this excerpt from "If We Must Die," McKay called for aggressive self-defense against the rioters:

> *If we must die, let it not be like hogs*
> *Hunted and penned in an inglorious spot,*
> *While round us bark the mad and hungry dogs,*
> *Making their mock at our accursed lot ...*
> *O kinsmen we must meet the common foe!*
> *Though far outnumbered let us show us brave,*
> *And for their thousand blows deal one deathblow!*
> *What though before us lies the open grave?*
> *Like men we'll face the murderous, cowardly pack,*
> *Pressed to the wall, dying, but fighting back!* [3]

McKay, who was 30 at the time the poem was published, expressed similar sentiments in his book *Harlem Shadows*, which

Claude McKay was one of many Harlem Renaissance writers who became famous.

includes more than 60 poems. This book made McKay the most celebrated black poet in the United States at the time.

Writing Songs

In the *New Republic* magazine, white critic Robert Littel discussed *Harlem Shadows*. He also acknowledged the talents of James Weldon Johnson. Littel concluded that the two authors "make me sit up and take notice when they write about their race and ours. They strike hard and pierce deep. It is not merely poetic emotions they express, but something fierce and constant, icy cold, and white hot."[4]

James Weldon Johnson was one of the most successful African American writers in the United States. Born in 1871, he enrolled in the all-black Atlanta University at the age of 16, and in 1897, he was the first black person to take the Florida Bar Exam to become a lawyer. Not long after that, Johnson began writing song lyrics with his brother, Rosamond, as a way to express their feelings about segregation in the South. The brothers traveled to New York in 1899 to sell their work, and within a few years, the Johnson brothers were a successful songwriting team. Songs such as "The Congo Love Song" and "Under the Bamboo Tree" were so popular that people bought hundreds of thousands of copies of the sheet music—the most common way for songs to be distributed to the public before records, cassette tapes, and CDs became widespread—making the Johnsons wealthy men. Their song "Lift Every Voice and Sing," about liberty bringing a new day after the dark night of slavery, became an instant classic. Written in 1900 to commemorate the day President Abraham Lincoln was born, the song became known as the "Negro National Hymn" or "Negro National Anthem" and is still widely sung today.

In 1912, Johnson published the novel *The Autobiography of an Ex-Colored Man* about a light-skinned black man who passes himself off as white, marries a white woman, and has two children. The plot was extremely controversial for the time, and Johnson published it anonymously so white people would not target him for violence.

Like Du Bois described in *The Souls of Black Folk*, the protagonist in Johnson's book is filled with self-doubt about his African American identity. He rejects his identity after witnessing a lynching,

James Weldon Johnson's
novel, *The Autobiography
of an Ex-Colored Man*, was
controversial partially because
it featured an interracial couple,
which was illegal at the time.

ashamed that he belongs to a race that could be treated in such a manner. However, after reading books by Frederick Douglass and other black inspirational figures, the character comes to appreciate black culture, with its musical and storytelling traditions. The plot takes an autobiographical turn when the character, like Johnson, becomes a composer and ragtime piano player, writing songs that blend American music with black spiritual traditions to present a positive image of African Americans to the world.

Although *The Autobiography of an Ex-Colored Man* was only popular with a small audience when it was published, Johnson continued to write fiction, nonfiction, and poetry. As editor of the newspaper *New York Age*, he wrote the influential "Views and Reviews" column between 1915 and 1923. During this period, Johnson published *The Book of American Negro Poetry* with the works of 31 black poets, most of whom were unknown at the time. In the preface to the book, Johnson stated that stereotypes of black inferiority could be easily disproved with increased awareness of black people's contributions to the arts. He believed that the way to measure the greatness of a culture was to look at how much art and literature it put out into the world, and he was determined to call the white public's attention to the large amount of such works black people had already produced and were continuing to produce.

Johnson wrote about black contributions to music, including spirituals, ragtime, and dance crazes. He also wrote about 19th-century black folktales and poetry. Johnson's overall theme—that black music, dance, and literature would undermine racism—was one of the guiding forces behind the Harlem Renaissance.

Writing for White Audiences

Several black writers of the Harlem Renaissance became quite popular in the 1920s; however, their books were published by a white New York literary establishment for white audiences. Therefore, many African American authors had to consider the racial prejudices of their white readers to be successful. In his 1928 essay, "The Dilemma of the Negro Author," Johnson explained the issue:

If the Negro author selects white America as his audience he is

THEY MADE HISTORY: JESSIE FAUSET

Jessie Fauset was born in New Jersey on April 27, 1882, and was raised in Philadelphia, Pennsylvania. Unlike many black women at the time, she received a college education; she wanted to attend Bryn Mawr College, but the school had no black students at the time and did not want to accept her. Instead, Bryn Mawr helped her get a scholarship to Cornell University, from which she graduated in 1905. She wanted to be a teacher in Philadelphia, but again she was denied because of her race. Instead, she found teaching positions in Baltimore, Maryland, as well as in Washington, DC.

At the age of 30, Fauset started writing for W. E. B. Du Bois's magazine *The Crisis*, and seven years later, he hired her as the literary editor. In this position, she encouraged many other Harlem Renaissance writers, helping them hone their skills and giving them exposure through publication. She also wrote four novels. The first two, *There Is Confusion* and *Plum Bun*, were well received. However, her last two, *The Chinaberry Tree* and *Comedy: American Style,* were less successful, as readers started to lose interest in the middle-class settings in which she placed her characters.

In 1929, the year *Plum Bun* came out, Fauset married a businessman named Herbert Harris. After his death in 1958, she moved from their home in New Jersey back to Philadelphia, where she died in 1961. Although she did not live in Harlem, Fauset's work with *The Crisis* and her own writing were important parts of the cultural movement known as the Harlem Renaissance.

bound to run up against ... a whole row of hard-set stereotypes which are not easily broken up. White America has some firm opinions as to what the Negro is, and consequently some pretty well fixed ideas as to what should be written about him, and how.

What is the Negro in the artistic conception of white America? In the brighter light, he is a simple, indolent, docile, improvident peasant; a singing, dancing, laughing weeping child; picturesque beside his log cabin and in the snowy fields of cotton; naïvely charming with his banjo and his songs in the moonlight and along the lazy Southern rivers; a faithful, ever-smiling and genuflecting old servitor to the white folks of quality; a pathetic and pitiable figure …

Ninety-nine one-hundredths of all that has been written about the Negro in the United States in three centuries and read with any degree of interest or pleasure by white America has been written in conformity to one or more of these ideas.[5]

However, not all black writers were concerned only with achieving success and fame. Many wrote to rebel against these stereotypes and tell their truth, presenting a more accurate, nuanced picture of black people and their culture—regardless of how many copies they sold. For example, in 1924, a major publishing house released Jessie Fauset's book, *There Is Confusion*, which depicts the lives of middle-class African American families from a woman's perspective. Fauset's characters are based on the world she knew. They had been in the United States for many generations, were somewhat affluent, and, like many white families of that era, placed great importance on class, pedigree, and manners. Fauset based her novel on her belief that middle-class black and white Americans shared more cultural similarities than was widely acknowledged. One publisher who had rejected *There Is Confusion* scoffed, "White readers just don't expect Negroes to be like this."[6]

Dialect: Avoid or Embrace?

Although he promoted black literature, Johnson believed that black authors should avoid writing in black dialect, or speech patterns, because black people were frequently judged as uneducated for using it. This dialect was the stereotypical speech of poor southern black Americans, who said things such as "gwine" instead of "going," "ma" instead of "my," and "mo" instead of "more."

Langston Hughes clashed with some of the other Harlem Renaissance writers because of his realistic portrayals of black urban life and his use of dialect in his poems.

While some authors believed that using black dialect degraded black people, many of Harlem's intellectual writers thought otherwise. Langston Hughes, who has been called a jazz poet because of the rhythmic, moving character of his words, made a name for himself writing in dialect. Hughes's first major poem, "The Weary Blues," won first prize in the poetry competition held by the literary magazine *Opportunity: A Journal of Negro Life* in 1925. This excerpt describes a man listening to an old blues musician in Harlem:

> *I heard that Negro sing, that old piano moan—*
> *"Ain't got nobody in all this world,*
> *Ain't got nobody but ma self.*
> *I's gwine to quit ma frownin'*
> *And put ma troubles on the shelf."* [7]

Reviewers loved "The Weary Blues" and Hughes's first book of poetry, but his second book of poems, *Fine Clothes to the Jew*, was highly criticized. The title, which upset Jewish people, refers to a man who is so poor he has to pawn his suit for a few nickels. The main criticism, however, came from the black community because of the way Hughes portrayed the reality of black urban life. As Hughes recalled in his 1940 autobiography, *The Big Sea*, black critics called the book "a disgrace to the race, a return to the dialect tradition, and a parading of all our racial defects before the public."[8] Black people, Hughes said, wanted literature to show the best representation of themselves; they knew white people already had a low opinion of them, and many felt that depicting black people and culture as anything other than sophisticated, intelligent, and upstanding was simply reinforcing those stereotypes.

In his defense, Hughes argued that while he sympathized with the critics' point of view, he did not know anybody who was "wholly beautiful and wholly good."[9] As he was not rich, he did not know what life was like for upper-class black Americans, such as those who attended elite universities and listened to classical music. Instead of writing about those people, he wrote about his life and the people who populated it.

PAST MEETS PRESENT: WHEN THEY SEE US

Today, presenting harsh realities about African American life is no longer as discouraged as it was in Hughes's time. Instead, works that do this are often seen as a way to show white people that racism still exists, even if they do not see it around them or experience it themselves. In 2019, the Netflix miniseries *When They See Us* premiered and accomplished just that. The series tells the story of the young men who were labeled the Central Park Five: five black and Latino teens who were wrongfully convicted of assaulting a white female jogger in New York City's Central Park in 1989 and spent years in jail for a crime they did not commit.

When They See Us received widespread praise from critics and viewers alike, but at the same time, many white viewers reported feeling extreme discomfort as they watched the way the boys were treated. At the time the case was being decided in court, the media reported on it in a way that dehumanized the teens. Seeing the miniseries, which makes a point of humanizing each character, makes the tragedy feel much more personal. In an article for the *Odyssey*, writer Lexi Locke told viewers,

> I don't want to hear, "It's too sad to watch. It makes me uncomfortable." If it makes you uncomfortable, then that means you are feeling and learning—feeling what Korey, Antron, Raymond, Yusef, and Kevin felt in 1989. Learning about something that the history books didn't teach you. Learning about yourself and waking up to see that what happened to those five boys—now men—is still *happening to black boys today in 2019.*[1]

1. Lexi Locke, "'When They See Us' SHOULD Make You Uncomfortable, That's All the More Reason to Watch It," *Odyssey*, June 10, 2019, www.theodysseyonline.com/watch-when-they-see-us.

Hughes was not the only writer to face criticism about this issue. The Harlem Renaissance was a period that was particularly sensitive for black authors. For the first time, the powerful New York publishing world was paying close attention, and there was much soul-searching among authors as to how they portrayed black people.

An Important Dinner

Writer and editor Charles S. Johnson hoped to address the perception gap between the black and white communities by planning a banquet to celebrate the publication of Fauset's first novel, *There Is Confusion*. This book showed the similarities between white and black families that had experienced similar levels of economic success. Johnson was editor of *Opportunity: A Journal of Negro Life*, the official publication of the National Urban League (NUL), an organization founded to help advance the economic interests of black Americans.

On March 21, 1924, Johnson hosted the NUL Civic Club Dinner. Hughes, James Weldon Johnson, and poet Countee Cullen were honored along with Fauset. Charles S. Johnson also invited white writers, editors, and critics from New York's powerful literary establishment. This event, attended by more than 100 people, stimulated great interest in black writers among white publishers and is considered the formal launching of the Harlem literary renaissance.

Paul U. Kellogg, one of the attendees at the Civic Club Dinner, was editor of the *Survey Graphic*, a popular illustrated magazine that focused on poverty, racism, education, working conditions, political reform, and other social issues. Inspired by the blossoming black literary movement, Kellogg decided to devote the entire March 1925 issue of the magazine to the art and literature of Harlem. The "Harlem Issue" was edited by writer, philosopher, and educator Alain Locke and remains one of the most detailed accounts of that era. The issue was so successful that Locke expanded it into a book, *The New Negro*, which explored the Harlem Renaissance's writing, art, and literary criticism.

Zora Neale Hurston is one of the most recognizable names and faces of the Harlem Renaissance.

Catching Fire

As the Harlem Renaissance progressed, other important voices emerged. One of the most vivacious, or energetic, members of the group, Zora Neale Hurston, was a latecomer to the renaissance. Historians say Hurston was born in 1891 in Notasulga, Alabama, but she claimed to be 10 years younger and born in Eatonville, Florida. During the 1920s, Hurston was known more for her humor, use of old-style slave dialect, and outsized charm than her literary accomplishments. Most of her critically acclaimed work was written in the 1930s, after the end of the Harlem Renaissance.

Hurston contributed several short stories to magazines while attending Barnard College, and people began to take notice of her work. After moving to Harlem in 1925, the independent, outspoken woman with a rich, commanding voice quickly became a central figure among the Harlem literary scene.

Stories of Hurston's exploits are legendary. She smoked cigarettes in public, which was considered disgraceful for a woman at the time. She also lived in a house full of men, including other writers and artists, which many considered scandalous. The members of the house were further criticized for throwing wild, drunken parties.

In 1926, Hurston collaborated with Wallace Thurman, Richard Nugent, and painter Aaron Douglas on the magazine *Fire!!*. Although short-lived, the magazine was the only publication of the Harlem Renaissance produced by the movement's artists and writers.

According to Langston Hughes, the group chose the title *Fire!!* because they wanted to "burn up a lot of the old, dead conventional Negro-white ideas of the past."[10] It featured articles mocking and scorning the literary establishment, celebrating jazz and blues music, and discussing forbidden topics such as homosexuality and pagan beliefs. Older black intellectuals, such as Du Bois, were shocked by the unseemly tone of the magazine.

The magazine was not profitable; each issue cost the equivalent of $4,000 to produce, and it was nearly impossible to get white magazine dealers to distribute it. Ironically, the magazine came to an end when the copies were destroyed by a fire that swept through the apartment where they were stored. Many of the black writers who had contributed to *Fire!!* went on to have respectable careers as authors, poets, and educators. Hardened in the fires of prejudice, segregation, and disappointment, they provided a unique perspective on black life in the United States for generations to come. The impact and influence of *Fire!!* is clearly evidenced in the fact that, in January 2017, the magazine was revived and reissued with the new title *FIYAH*. The magazine's website lists its mission as follows:

> *What does it mean to be Black and look at the intersectional issues of equality through the lens of science fiction and fantasy? …*
>
> *FIYAH rises from the ashes of the Black literary tradition started by* Fire!! *in 1926. We aren't here for respectability. We're here to ask what it means to be Black and extraordinary. We are a place to showcase your stories and grow your career … we know you have stories to tell and we are here for it.*[11]

However, as with *Fire!!*, *FIYAH* has run into problems. While *Fire!!* was outright scorned by black and white critics, some people believe that the targeting of the new magazine has been more subtle. In September 2018, the website Book Riot reported that all the issues of *FIYAH* had been removed from the website Goodreads. Similarly, the issues of a literary magazine called *Anathema*, which showcases fiction by people of color and LGBTQ+ writers, had been removed. Both magazines can still be read by purchasing a subscription through their respective websites, but putting them on Goodreads allowed more people to learn about these publications. Many believed the removal of these two magazines pointed to bias among the Goodreads librarians. The librarians responded that, according to Goodreads policy, magazines should not be on the website, as it is a catalogue for books; however, on its own website, Goodreads states that literary magazines are considered to be the same as books. This confusion about the policy and the noticeable removal of two magazines showcasing writers of color—while other magazines remained on the website—caused many people to suspect that racism was the main motivation. This incident shows that, although society has come a long way since the 1920s, there is still more work to be done. Furthermore, it proves that, like the writers of the Harlem Renaissance, modern-day writers of color are determined to persist and speak up regardless of any resistance they encounter.

How You See History

1. Why do you think so many black people at this time felt torn between their African and American heritages?

2. Why was Langston Hughes's use of dialect controversial?

3. Do you think white people's view of writing about black experiences has changed over the years? If so, in what ways has it changed?

CHAPTER THREE

MUSIC

Some types of art created during the Harlem Renaissance were considered "high art." This described literature, paintings, plays, and other works that were aimed at intellectuals. The goal of high art was to make people think and challenge their preconceived opinions.

However, not all artists considered themselves intellectuals. Some simply wanted to have fun and enrich people's everyday lives. The kind of art they created, which came to be called "low art," revolved around loud, wild jazz and blues that was played in speakeasies (hidden, illegal establishments that sold liquor during the Prohibition era, when alcohol was outlawed), dance halls, and after-hours clubs. Both high and low art had value, but low art tended to be judged much more harshly and was frequently associated in people's minds with drug and alcohol use—despite the fact that many intellectuals used these substances as well.

Authors and poets of the time, who were often called literati, frequently sneered at jazz and blues music, believing that it perpetuated negative stereotypes about black people. Harlem Renaissance musicians were amused by this opinion and sometimes even included the snobbish literati in their song lyrics.

Jazz and blues musicians such as the ones shown here were very popular in the 1920s, especially in Harlem.

Some critics felt the music was a modern version of the racist minstrel shows from the 19th century. In these shows, black or white entertainers performed in blackface, which was theatrical makeup or burnt cork that gave the appearance of dark skin. Black performers even had to wear blackface makeup on the stage because white audiences would not watch them without it. These minstrel shows mocked black people by portraying them as lazy, superstitious, and only good for playing music or dancing.

Jazz and Prohibition

The literati were in the minority; most people enjoyed jazz. In fact, it was so popular that another term for the 1920s is the Jazz Age. The word "jazz" was originally a black slang term for sexual intercourse, but it became part of the American lexicon during the Roaring Twenties. Fashionable clothes were called "jazz dresses," and modern syncopated verse was called "jazz poetry." However, first and foremost, jazz was the music that was heard everywhere in Harlem. It floated out of radios and record players in barbershops and beauty parlors. It was performed by live bands at dance halls, cabarets, and clubs. Soon, Harlem's sound was attracting white visitors to the area, including celebrities.

It wasn't just the music that brought white visitors to Harlem. In January 1919, the 18th Amendment to the US Constitution was ratified, prohibiting the manufacture, sale, or transportation of alcoholic beverages beginning in 1920. The law, commonly known as Prohibition, profoundly influenced American life—not because it worked, but because it failed spectacularly and led to a thriving underground culture. Instead of giving up alcohol, as the law intended, people simply began illegally making their own. However, drinking homemade alcohol was frequently dangerous and could result in blindness or death. Instead of risking it, some people chose to do business with criminals who imported, or bootlegged, whiskey and beer from Canada and elsewhere. It was sold in secret, hidden clubs called speakeasies, many of which were run by organized crime groups.

With the price of a forbidden drink soaring from 25 cents in 1920 to $2 in 1925, running a speakeasy could be very profitable. The secretive nature of these clubs and the lure of alcohol attracted adventurous young white people who spent freely and danced to jazz music.

With a steady flow of wealthy customers, Harlem was booming with speakeasies, cellars, lounges, cafes, taverns, and supper clubs. Because white people wanted to visit these establishments, the African American character of Harlem quickly changed. The white visitors to Harlem did not represent the average American. Some said these customers were afflicted by "Harlemania," a term coined to describe a nearly hysterical love of the

During Prohibition, wealthy white people flocked to Harlem to drink in speakeasies similar to the one shown here.

The Cotton Club was one of the most popular nightclubs in New York City. Although black people were hired to work there, they were not allowed to go there as customers.

area. Among those visiting Harlem in their expensive cars were Gertrude Vanderbilt Whitney (great-granddaughter of railroad tycoon Cornelius Vanderbilt and founder of the Whitney Museum of American Art); French princess Violette Murat; German-born financier Otto Kahn; movie star Harold Lloyd; and Lady Patricia Mountbatten, the wife of British naval commander Lord Mountbatten. These people not only visited the "high" art establishments but also went "slumming" by going to "low-down" speakeasies.

One of the complications of this attention from high society was that, due to segregation laws, black Americans were banned from eating at several of the best restaurants, where only the staff and entertainers were black. A typical example was the gangster-owned Cotton Club, the country's most famous nightclub. Located on Harlem's Lenox Avenue, the Cotton Club denied black people entry unless they were entertaining all-white crowds.

Many black people resented the white invasion of their neighborhood and their resulting exclusion. According to Langston Hughes,

> Harlem Negroes did not like the Cotton Club and never appreciated its Jim Crow policy in the very heart of their dark community. Nor did ordinary Negroes like the growing influx of whites toward Harlem after sundown, flooding the little cabarets and bars where formerly only colored people laughed and sang, and where now the strangers were given the best ringside tables to sit and stare at the Negro customers—like amusing animals in a zoo.[1]

Piano Music

The Harlem Renaissance offered steady employment to many talented black musicians and singers. There were at least 15 major jazz bands and 100 lesser-known ensembles that played in the neighborhood throughout the Roaring Twenties. These musicians were from all over the United States, and they helped create the true Harlem jazz sound.

The roots of jazz can be traced to late-19th-century New Orleans, Louisiana, where black musicians blended several forms

FROM THE SOURCE: RENT PARTIES

Many residents of Harlem were unable to afford the expensive clubs patronized by white clientele and the Talented Tenth; in fact, some could barely afford the rent on their apartment. For this reason, "rent parties" became common, where attendees would crowd into an apartment and contribute anywhere from 10 to 50 cents toward the host's rent. The parties lasted until dawn, and the entertainment could be spectacular. One of Harlem's leading piano players, Willie "the Lion" Smith, described playing at one of these rent parties:

Piano players called these affairs jumps or shouts ... It got so we never stopped and we were up and down Fifth, Seventh, and Lenox all night long hitting the keys ... On a single Saturday [we would] book as many as three parties ...

There were, of course, some of the chitterling struts [parties] where a bunch of pianists would be in competition. [Our booking agent] Lippy was a great promoter and was always trying to steam up the guests to argue who was the best ... you had to stay by the keyboard to hold your own reputation for being a fast pianist ... During [the] early hours close to dawn the ... lights would be dimmed down and the people would call out to the piano player. "Play it, oh, play it," or "Break it down," or "Get in the gully and give us the everlovin' stomp." Those were happy days.[1]

1. Quoted in Jervis Anderson, *This Was Harlem* (New York, NY: Farrar Straus and Giroux, 1982), pp. 155–56.

of traditional music, including work songs, blues, Mardi Gras marches, European military music, and ragtime to create a completely new sound. Ragtime was particularly favored in Harlem. In this style, pianists play complicated songs with the right hand, "tickling" the keys with the melody, while the left hand plays a complex section on the bass end.

Scott Joplin was considered the king of ragtime. His 1899 composition "Maple Leaf Rag" was the first instrumental music piece to sell more than 1 million copies of sheet music. Joplin moved to Harlem in 1907, and his music evolved into the "stride piano" style. The sound was so large and powerful that it could be compared to listening to a full orchestra. Joplin died in 1917, before the official start of the Harlem Renaissance.

The piano players gave each other nicknames, such as "Bear," "Beetle," "Beast," and "Brute." Harlem's most famous were Willie "the Lion" Smith, Ferdinand "Jelly Roll" Morton, and Fats Waller. New Jersey-born pianist James P. Johnson perfected the "stride piano" style in Harlem and earned the title "Father of Stride Piano." In addition to being a pianist, Johnson was a composer who wrote 230 songs, 19 symphonic works, and 11 musicals. His most famous composition was "The Charleston," which had an accompanying dance. This song brought jazz to a wider audience and became synonymous with the Jazz Age.

Johnson often participated in contests with other notable stride players. These events, in which pianists attempted to cut each other down, or outplay each other with nearly impossible riffs and runs, attracted many young musicians. Among them was up-and-coming pianist Edward "Duke" Ellington, who was awed by Johnson's creative licks, fast hands, and precision runs.

Ellington was born in Washington, DC, in 1899 and moved to Harlem in 1923. Within a few years, he formed a red-hot band called the Washingtonians. Trumpet player Bubber Miley gave the Washingtonians a unique voice, wringing a down-and-dirty, blues-drenched, "gut bucket" sound from his horn. Ellington called it the "Jungle Sound," and it came to represent Harlem jazz.

By 1927, Ellington was pioneering a new type of jazz, composing music that mixed jazz with the lush orchestral sounds heard in popular theatrical musicals. By adding strings, brass, and woodwinds, Ellington forged a distinctive sound. Because Ellington's grand sound appealed to an upper-class white audience, critics called it "sophisticated music."

The Charleston became a national dance craze. Shown here are young Harlem residents dancing the Charleston.

Ellington's new sound developed around the time his group was hired as the house band for the Cotton Club. The fashionable club was decorated in the style of a 19th-century southern mansion, and the black employees were offensively portrayed as either slaves on a plantation or as savages in the jungle. These exclusionary and highly offensive policies reinforced stereotypes about black people.

The Washingtonians, now renamed Duke Ellington and His Cotton Club Orchestra, quickly achieved national recognition when the band was featured on CBS radio broadcasts live from the club every Saturday night. With his newfound fame and money, Ellington was able to hire the best musicians in New York and write stunning arrangements that allowed them to showcase their talents.

Ellington played at the Cotton Club off and on until 1933. Between 1927 and 1931, his orchestra made 150 records. When not playing and recording in New York, Ellington toured extensively in the United States and Europe. Ellington's many memorable compositions, including "Mood Indigo," "It Don't Mean a Thing if It Ain't Got That Swing," and "Sophisticated Lady," made use of catchy and unusual melodies. Although his strutting, swinging sounds became jazz classics across the globe, Ellington's music was firmly rooted in Harlem. In one essay, the late music professor Mark Tucker wrote that even when he was far from home, "Ellington continued to celebrate Harlem in music. His compositions described its echoes and air shafts, boys and blue belles [beautiful women]. His songs advised people to drop off there and to slap their soles on Seventh Avenue. His signature piece even told them which train to take [to reach Harlem]."[2]

Bessie Smith and the Blues

In addition to being segregated, the price of a night at the Cotton Club was out of reach for the average Harlem

THEY MADE HISTORY: GLADYS BENTLEY

In an era when women were more severely restrained by gender roles, Gladys Bentley made waves. The Harlem Renaissance was a more liberal era than the ones that came before or after it, and LGBTQ+ culture flourished, but Bentley still stood out. The *New York Times* explained, "In her top hat and tuxedo, Bentley belted gender-bending original blues numbers and lewd [dirty] parodies of popular songs ... When not accompanying herself with a dazzling piano, the mightily built singer often swept through the audience, flirting with women in the crowd."[1]

Bentley realized she was a lesbian at a young age; she recalled her parents worrying about her attraction to women even when she was a child. She was born in Trinidad and raised in Philadelphia, but at age 16, she moved to Harlem and began performing. She quickly became a celebrity, earning enough money to rent an expensive apartment on Park Avenue, hire multiple servants, and buy a luxury car. In one interview, she told reporters that she had married a white woman, but her wife's identity was never made public.

Bentley's popularity decreased during and after the Great Depression, when society again grew less tolerant of the LGBTQ+ community. In 1937, she left New York for San Francisco, California, and although she continued to be a sought-after performer, club owners sometimes required her to wear skirts instead of her trademark tuxedo. For this reason, she performed more often at Mona's 440 Club, the first lesbian bar in San Francisco, where she felt more comfortable. In the 1950s, when laws targeting the LGBTQ+ community began to be enforced, Bentley started wearing dresses all the time, and twice she publicly announced that she had married men, although one of the men she claimed to have married denied this. She died from complications of the flu at the age of 52.

1. Giovanni Russonello, "Gladys Bentley," *New York Times*, accessed November 6, 2019, www.nytimes.com/interactive/2019/obituaries/gladys-bentley-overlooked.html.

Gladys Bentley resisted gender norms for most of her career by performing in men's clothing.

resident, as it was equal to a week's wages. Instead, they could find a wealth of entertainment in the "Jungle Alley" district. In *Harlem Speaks*, Cary D. Wintz described the district:

> [Jungle Alley] provided a variety of entertainment options and a more eclectic and risqué environment. It catered to a racially mixed and ... uninhibited clientele. In Jungle Alley everyone rubbed shoulders—gay and straight, whites from across the city,

working-class blacks as well as intellectuals, writers, musicians, artists, businessmen, criminals, and prostitutes. They drank bootleg liquor, had access to marijuana and harder drugs, and danced or just listened to jazz and blues artists, often until daybreak.[3]

Singer Gladys Bentley was a typical entertainer in the district. Working at the Clam House, the vocalist sang suggestive songs while wearing a man's top hat and tuxedo. She sat at her piano from 10 p.m. until dawn, playing blues classics without stopping. Bentley eventually became so popular she moved to bigger Harlem clubs, and then to California. She was only one of several Harlem blues singers to achieve international fame. Bessie Smith, known as "the Empress of the Blues," was also among the biggest stars of the Harlem Renaissance. Smith, Bentley, and other female singers of the era often used their song lyrics to criticize the patriarchy and male feelings of entitlement, or being owed something.

Bessie Smith was born into dire poverty around 1892 in Chattanooga, Tennessee. She was orphaned by age nine and earned a meager living dancing and singing on street corners, accompanied by her brother on guitar. As a teenager, Smith was hired as a professional dancer in a black touring show whose star was the legendary singer Gertrude "Ma" Rainey, nicknamed "Mother of the Blues."

During an era when many black women were treated with even less respect than black men, Rainey carried herself as a proud diva. She sang about her life—bad times, relationship problems, and crippling loneliness—but demanded respect from her audiences. Smith gained Rainey's admiration, and the two became inseparable, performing and writing songs together. By the early 1920s, both were major stars, playing together in theaters packed with integrated audiences.

In the early 1920s, most record companies refused to record black artists. However, after blues singer Mamie Smith (no relation to Bessie) had a few unexpected hits, record companies realized there was a huge demand for what they called "race records." Bessie Smith recorded "Down Hearted Blues" in 1923,

PAST MEETS PRESENT: CHRISTONE "KINGFISH" INGRAM

Blues was invented and popularized by black musicians, but after it became popular, many white musicians started playing in that style as well. White musicians such as Johnny Winter, Paul Butterfield, and Stevie Ray Vaughan became so famous for their blues music that some people stopped associating black people with the genre.

Many people are also surprised when a young person today is interested in the blues, since it is not a modern music style. When Christone "Kingfish" Ingram learned about the musicians who had made blues popular, he started taking guitar lessons and eventually began performing live. At the age of 19, he became famous thanks to his YouTube videos; he even appeared on the second season of the Netflix show *Luke Cage*. In 2018, *Rolling Stone* featured him in an article, calling him "the latest blues savior."[1] Ingram said he has encountered racism from people who are surprised to see a young black man performing the blues. He told *Rolling Stone*, "I've actually had times when people thought I was like part of the crew or something like that ... This is our culture, man. It's part of our history just as much as jazz and rap."[2]

1. Brian Hiatt, "Is Christone 'Kingfish' Ingram the Future of the Blues?," *Rolling Stone*, October 31, 2018, www.rollingstone.com/music/music-features/christone-kingfish-ingram-future-blues-747484.

2. Quoted in Hiatt, "Is Christone 'Kingfish' Ingram the Future of the Blues?"

and the record sold an astounding 780,000 copies that year. The money saved Columbia Records, which was nearly bankrupt, but Smith was only paid $250. In contrast, popular white artists such as Al Jolson were paid a royalty for each record sold and quickly became millionaires. Although her following records sold millions, Smith primarily made her fortune as a performer, earning

The Savoy remained a popular spot well after the Harlem Renaissance ended. Shown here is a couple swing dancing at the Savoy in 1947.

up to $2,000 per week playing various theaters in cities such as New York and Chicago.

Many in Harlem respected Smith. However, due to her lifestyle, the Harlem literati, who equated culture with European classical music and opera, shunned her. According to jazz critic Chip Deffa, upper-class black Americans considered Smith "too much of the streets, a rough-edged reminder of lower-class roots they wanted to forget ... Smith was a crude, primitive 'blues shouter' to be ignored."[4] Smith recognized these attitudes and responded in the 1933 song "Gimme a Pigfoot (and a Bottle of Beer)." In the lyrics, Smith scolded the literati for being snobby and for dismissing the blues.

By this time, Smith's career was beginning to suffer; as the economic collapse known as the Great Depression showed no signs of letting up, most people were more concerned with buying food than with buying records. When Smith recorded with jazz greats Jack Teagarden, Benny Goodman, and Chu Berry, however, she began moving beyond the blues and taking jazz in a new direction.

A Diverse Spot

With her low-down blues, Smith had difficulty competing with the lively jazz music that attracted massive crowds to the Savoy Ballroom, Harlem's hottest nightspot, which opened in March 1926. Built by a white music promoter and a black businessman, the Savoy was an architectural wonder, featuring a huge lobby and a block-long dance hall atop two dazzling, mirror-lined marble staircases.

The dance palace was described as a community ballroom where anyone—black or white, rich or poor, local or tourist—could gain admission for only 50 cents on most nights and 75 cents on Sundays. In addition to drawing Harlem's blue-collar crowd of busboys, truck drivers, and domestic workers, the Savoy attracted royalty and movie stars, including the Prince of Wales, Marlene Dietrich, Greta Garbo, and Lana Turner. On weekends, up to 4,000 guests packed into the club to hear the bands play and to dance.

Fletcher Henderson and his Rainbow Orchestra were one of the world-class acts that played at the Savoy. Another star was drummer Chick Webb, leader of the Chick Webb Orchestra. Webb's driving beat was compared to a railroad train running at full throttle. The Savoy sponsored the Battle of the Bands, where guest bands from New York, Chicago, and New Orleans were pitted against Webb's band. Even jazz greats such as Louis Armstrong, Cab Calloway, King Oliver, and Fess Williams feared battling Webb, who was often judged the winner by the cheering crowd.

Some of the best entertainment at the Savoy came from the dancers who strutted and jumped on the famous 50 by 250 foot (15 by 76 m) dance floor. The floor was used so much that it had to be replaced every three years. Many of the dance fads that swept across the country in the 1920s, such as the Lindy Hop, the Suzy Q, and the Shim Sham Shimmy, were invented at the Savoy, the "Home of Happy Feet."

On Tuesday nights, the club hosted the Savoy 400, featuring professional dancers such as George "Shorty" Snowden, who is often credited with naming the Lindy Hop. The Lindy Hop included pinwheel spins and "breakaways" in which the female dance partner was thrown and twirled high in the air. Swing dancers still perform the Lindy Hop today.

On Thursday nights, women were admitted free to the Savoy for "Kitchen Mechanics' Night," a slang term for cooks and maids. Saturday night was known as "Square Night" and was designed for the "unhip" white downtowners who showed up to crowd the dance floor.

The musicians who played at the Savoy and all the other musicians of the Harlem Renaissance achieved two historically important goals. First, they introduced entirely new styles of playing and types of music to the world. Second, they gave black and white Americans the chance to get to know each other in an entertaining and relaxed venue. This helped bridge—and then tear down—social and racial barriers. Supporting black culture, including art, literature, theater, and music, became fashionable among wealthy white people. Driven by the percussion and power of jazz music, the Harlem Renaissance reached a wider audience and made a permanent mark on the Roaring Twenties.

How You See History

1. Why do you think people made a distinction between "high art" and "low art"? What do you think these terms mean?

2. Why is blackface racist?

3. Why do you think the Harlem literati thought European music was more cultured than jazz and blues?

CHAPTER FOUR

THEATER

During the Harlem Renaissance, black people made famous contributions to every major art form, and theater was no exception. On May 23, 1921, the musical revue *Shuffle Along* opened at the 63rd Street Music Hall near Broadway. The show was filled with comedy, ragtime music, and jazz dancing, and it ran for an astounding number of performances—at least 484, according to the Broadway Playbill website. It was the first major production in years to be produced, written, and performed entirely by black people, but it was popular with white audiences as well. In fact, so many white people attended the show that police were forced to convert 63rd Street into a one-way street to cope with the increased traffic. This type of excitement and positive attention marked an enormous change from the way white people had previously viewed black theatrical works.

By Black People, for Black People

Shuffle Along was one of the earliest black-produced theater shows to become a hit with all audiences, but black theater was far from new. As early as 1910, black playwrights wrote dramas, comedies, and musicals for upper-class black audiences who could afford the tickets to Broadway shows but were either not allowed into the theaters or had to sit in the segregated balcony seats.

In the 1920s, plays, musicals, and movies starring black actors, such as Clarence Muse, became more popular than ever before.

With black actors, dancers, and singers also largely banned on Broadway, Harlem productions attracted the most talented black performers in the United States. Many performed plays reflecting on the pain and beauty they had personally experienced. As David Krasner wrote in his book *A Beautiful Pageant*, "Black theatre explored community issues away from white audiences and the demand to please them."[1]

By 1914, there were several theaters in Harlem with their own repertory companies, or permanent groups of actors, directors, and stage technicians. The most famous, the Anita Bush Stock Company (later called the Lafayette Players), was founded by Lester Walton, amusement critic for *New York Age*, and Anita Bush, known as "the Little Mother of Negro Drama." The Lafayette Players presented a variety of entertainment, including musicals, comedies, grand operas, and William Shakespeare's plays. Their most popular productions, however, were uptown Harlem performances of downtown Broadway hits. These plays with all-black casts included classics such as *Dr. Jekyll and Mr. Hyde* and *The Count of Monte Cristo*. However, the play *Within the Law* was the one that attracted widespread attention when lawyer-turned-actor Clarence Muse mocked the common practice of white actors appearing in blackface makeup. Langston Hughes and Milton Meltzer explained:

> *Muse, who had enormous popularity with Harlem audiences and whose rich deep voice was well known, used a gimmick in [Within the Law] which never failed to bring the house down. At his initial entrance, Muse first began to speak off stage, carrying on a brief conversation while still out of sight. The audience would think, "There comes Clarence," but they were unprepared for what was to happen—the very dark Muse stepped on stage completely white. Astonished pandemonium always broke out. Applause shook the theatre.* Within the Law *in Harlem became an S.R.O. [standing room only] hit.*[2]

Muse later became a writer, director, and producer as well as one of the most famous black actors in Hollywood during the 1940s. However, Muse was just one among many fine actors in the company that included Abbie Mitchell, Laura Bowman, Charles Gilpin, Hilda Simms, and Frank Wilson. These actors were so talented that they began attracting white crowds from downtown.

The Lafayette Players honed their skills in Harlem, but in April 1917, many of them participated in another groundbreaking event when they appeared in *Three Plays for the Negro Theatre* at the Garden Theater on Broadway. The three one-act plays, written by white playwright Ridgely Torrence and produced with two white collaborators, featured an all-black cast of actors. James Weldon Johnson recalled the significance of this event in his 1930 book, *Black Manhattan*, writing that the opening of this performance was "the most important single event in the entire history of the Negro in the American theatre ... It was the first time anywhere in the United States the Negro actors in the dramatic theatre [commanded] the serious attention of the critics and of the general press and public."[3]

Three Plays for the Negro Theatre did not run for long because the day after it opened, the United States entered World War I. However, the production was a milestone: It was the first time black artists appeared in serious dramatic roles, showing complex human emotions in front of a white audience. It was viewed by the black community as a resounding rejection of the trivial humor and stereotypes perpetuated by old minstrel shows.

Offending Audiences

It took three years for another drama with a black cast to appear on Broadway. *The Emperor Jones*, written by white author Eugene O'Neill, tells the story of Brutus Jones, a convicted black murderer who escapes from prison. He travels to an unnamed island in the Caribbean, where he uses his skills as a con artist to become emperor.

The Emperor Jones starred Charles Gilpin. The play received criticism because his character speaks a crude black southern dialect, and his actions perpetuate a stereotypical view of the African American male as a crook and a dangerous criminal. Part of the way Gilpin fought against this portrayal was to change the dialogue—much to O'Neill's displeasure—using terms such as "black baby," "Negro," or

Dudley Digges (*left*) and Paul Robeson (*right*) are shown here in the 1933 movie version of *The Emperor Jones*.

"colored man" in place of offensive racial slurs.

Despite the criticism, *The Emperor Jones* was an overnight success after its November 1, 1920, premiere at the Provincetown Theatre off Broadway. Thousands of people wanted tickets, and lines reached around the block. As a result, the production was moved to a larger theater on Broadway and extra shows were added. For his role in the play, Gilpin was awarded the NAACP Spingarn Medal for the highest achievement of a black American.

White audiences had ignored the racial stereotypes in *The Emperor Jones*, but O'Neill's next play, *All God's Chillun Got Wings*, offended them. Starring black actor Paul Robeson and white actress Mary Blair, *All God's Chillun* was about interracial marriage and called for Blair to kiss Robeson's hand onstage. When the press was notified of this provocative storyline, many newspaper editorial boards demanded the play be banned. The news of the kiss outraged the public, and the cast was flooded with death threats. Although there was fear that riots would break out or the theater would be bombed, the debate only fueled demand for tickets. *All God's Chillun* opened peacefully in November 1924, and Robeson and Blair were catapulted to international stardom.

A Wider Audience

By the time *All God's Chillun* premiered, *Shuffle Along* was being performed by road companies in packed theaters across the United States. The play "legitimized the black musical, [spawned] dozens of imitators, [and made African American musicals] a Broadway staple,"[4] according to theater historian Allen Woll.

Despite its success, *Shuffle Along* faced an uphill struggle and almost failed to get on the stage. No black musical comedy had opened on Broadway since 1910, and those that premiered in earlier times had failed. As Lester A. Walton, editor of *New York Age*, explained in 1924, white promoters at the time *Shuffle Along* premiered would not produce black revues because "white amusement seekers would not patronize a colored show as a legitimate theatrical proposition. Negro entertainment [was regarded] merely as a lure for slumming parties [only suitable on] the fringe of the theatre district."[5]

The creators of *Shuffle Along* overcame these difficulties through sheer talent. Many of the cast had experience in vaudeville, which was a type of popular entertainment featuring singing, dancing, and comedy acts. Performers Flournoy Miller and Aubrey Lyles were known for their hilarious comedy routines on the vaudeville circuit. Writers Noble Sissle and Eubie Blake, known as the Dixie Duo, were also established vaudeville stars. Blake, the most famous of the crew, began playing the organ when he was 5 years old, composed "Charleston Rag" on the piano when he was 12, and was playing keyboards with Big Jim Europe's jazz band at 18. Blake had written most of the music for *Shuffle Along* with Sissle long before the play premiered. However, the Dixie Duo could not get white producers to buy their songs and publish them as sheet music, so they had no way to make money from them.

In 1920, the creators of *Shuffle Along* were struggling to produce a play that was conceived primarily for black audiences on Broadway, the most competitive entertainment environment in the world at that time. With no outside financing, they were forced to pay for rehearsals with their vaudeville salaries. Many of the actors, singers, and dancers worked for free, hoping for a payday when the show began playing. *Shuffle Along* opened first in Washington, DC, in early 1921. After two successful weeks and a short run in Philadelphia, the producers were able to take it to New York. Amazed that the show went on despite their nearly nonexistent budget, Blake later remarked:

> *I still don't know how we did it. We didn't have money for nothin'—not for train fare when we needed it, not for scenery. It just seemed that we found everything just when we needed it. I believe if something is meant to happen, it's going to happen. That's how we all felt! It was like watchin' new miracles every day.*[6]

The money shortage also meant that Blake and the others could not hire big-name stars. However, after the success of *Shuffle Along*, several of the singers and dancers found stardom. Josephine Baker became famous on Broadway and an international sensation nearly overnight after she appeared in the show's chorus line. Florence Mills, a cabaret singer and comic, was soon the top black star in America and went on to perform to critical acclaim in many European cities. Sheet music and records of songs from the revue also became worldwide hits, including "I'm Just Wild About Harry," "Bandana Days," "Love Will Find a Way," and "In Honeysuckle Time."

Blake also became a major star. During intermission on opening night, white audience members were so awed by him that they approached him just to touch his hand or coat sleeve. Commenting on this reaction, Blake stated, "It made me feel like, well, at last, I'm a human being."[7]

After the success of *Shuffle Along*, Sissle and Blake wrote other popular musicals, including *Chocolate Dandies*, which featured Baker. Blake also did solo projects, such as the musical

In 2016, *Shuffle Along* was revived for a limited time on Broadway. In addition to the original show's acts, the new version added a storyline about how the 1921 version was created and how it changed theater.

Blackbirds—featuring Mills, Ethel Waters, and dancer Bill "Bojangles" Robinson—and international hit songs such as "Diga Diga Doo" and "I Can't Give You Anything but Love." Other popular black revues that played Broadway in the wake of *Shuffle Along* included *Rang Tang*, *Keep Shufflin'*, and the Fats Waller production *Hot Chocolates*.

Showing Real Life

African American comedy revues were beloved by black and white audiences. However, some of the intellectuals behind the New Negro renaissance were appalled at seeing black comedians performing in heavy blackface makeup on Broadway. Despite the criticism of the literati crowd, successful black revues paved the way for a second wave of dramatic plays with black casts. Some of these shows, written mostly by white playwrights, were credited with accurately depicting black life in the United States.

In 1926, Paul Green's play *In Abraham's Bosom* opened at the

THEY MADE HISTORY: JOSEPHINE BAKER

Josephine Baker became an international star nearly overnight after first appearing in the chorus line of *Shuffle Along* at the age of 17. Baker, however, was not hired for her stunning beauty. Instead, she impressed the show's musical producer, Eubie Blake, with her comedic dance performances, doing things such as crossing her eyes, making faces, tripping, falling out of step with the other dancers, and humorously rushing to catch up. When she appeared before audiences, she quickly stole the show and was soon one of the most popular and well-paid members of the cast.

After a triumphant run in *Shuffle Along*, Baker appeared in *Chocolate Dandies*, but she could not endure American racism. In 1925, she fled Harlem and embarked on an extremely successful career in Paris. Her dance routines highlighted seemingly impossible contorted motions patterned on the movements of African animals. Off the stage, Baker made a stir parading down Paris streets with a pet leopard on a leash.

During World War II and the German occupation of France, Baker was a member of the French Resistance and worked with the Red Cross. After her 1956 retirement, she continued to perform occasionally until her death in 1975.

Provincetown Playhouse. It portrays a black farmer who struggles against society to obtain an education. In the end, he kills his white half-brother and is hanged by a mob. DuBose Heyward was another white author from the Carolinas who had viewed the plight of southern black Americans through sympathetic eyes. His 1925 novel, *Porgy*, tells the story of a disabled homeless man living in the fictitious Catfish Row area of Charleston, South Carolina. The year after it was published, Heyward's wife, Dorothy, an Ohio-born playwright, began adapting it for the stage. The play premiered at the Guild Theatre on Broadway on October 10, 1927, with a critically acclaimed black cast.

As black theatrical attractions gained the attention of the wealthier white public, prices rose and segregation laws were enforced. Just as most Harlem residents were not able to go to the Cotton Club, they were not able to see a performance of *Porgy*. The tickets were $25 each—a week's pay for an average Harlem resident—and moreover, the Guild was a segregated theater. So while Harlem's richest citizens were able to afford a ticket to *Porgy*, they were forced to sit in the "colored section" in the balcony. Regardless, many Harlem residents were proud of *Porgy* because of its strong ties to the neighborhood. Cast members such as Rose McClendon, who played Serena; Frank Wilson, who played Porgy; Evelyn Ellis, who played Bess; and Percy Verwayne, who played Sportin' Life, were well-known bohemians who hung around a Harlem club called Dark Tower. In addition, the street corners and storefront churches on *Porgy's* Catfish Row were based on director Rouben Mamoulian's tours through Harlem.

Porgy ran for 850 performances and was considered one of the greatest dramas of the Harlem Renaissance. It was remade in 1935 into the opera *Porgy and Bess*, with music by George Gershwin and lyrics by Ira Gershwin and Dorothy Heyward. *Porgy and Bess* was revived again in 1959 by MGM for a film version featuring an all-star black cast, including Sidney Poitier, Dorothy Dandridge, Sammy Davis Jr., Pearl Bailey, and Diahann Carroll.

Before starring in *Porgy*, Frank Wilson was a Harlem mailman who wrote plays in his spare time. After becoming a Broadway star, Wilson used his connections to produce a play he had written called *Meek Mose* and employ as many Harlem actors as he could. New York mayor Jimmy Walker addressed the crowd on opening night at the Princess Theater, and other politicians and members of the city's upper classes were in attendance. However, some people were upset by the stereotypes in the play, and most critics were not impressed. *Meek Mose* closed in less than a month.

By this time, a series of events had begun shaking the foundations of black theater on Broadway. In November 1927, Florence Mills died unexpectedly from acute appendicitis at the height of

DuBose Heyward's story about Porgy was incredibly popular in all its forms. Shown here is a cast of *Porgy and Bess* in the 1950s.

her fame. Meanwhile, Harlem Renaissance promoters Alain Locke, James Weldon Johnson, and W. E. B. Du Bois had moved on to new interests and were paying less attention to black theater and drama. More devastating, a new technology created irresistible competition for Broadway: movies. In 1927, silent movies came to an end when feature films began including sound. These "talkies" drew audiences, actors, and writers away from live theater, and attendance fell dramatically.

Then, in October 1929, a massive stock market crash signaled the beginning of the Great Depression. Four months later, *The Green Pastures* opened at the Mansfield Theater. *The Green Pastures*, written by white author Marc Connelly, focused on black tales of spirituality

PAST MEETS PRESENT: BLACK PANTHER

Movie-making technology was not widely available during the Harlem Renaissance, but today it has become easier for black writers and directors to tell their stories onscreen. Over the years, there have been many movies featuring mainly black casts, some of which were written or directed by black people. These include *Moonlight*, *Hidden Figures*, *12 Years a Slave*, and *Us*, just to name a few. Many of these have received praise as well as criticism. One recent example is the Marvel movie *Black Panther*.

As the Marvel Cinematic Universe has exploded in popularity in recent years, *Black Panther* had a high budget for promotion and was eagerly awaited by fans of both the Marvel movies and comics. However, the movie received mixed reviews from some viewers. Many black people were excited to watch a movie with a majority-black cast, set in a world where black people had made great technological strides without the interference or help of white people. The hashtag #WhatBlackPantherMeansToMe started trending on Twitter, allowing black people to share their delight that the characters in the movie were intelligent and capable, as opposed to other movies where they had frequently been portrayed as criminals or sidekicks to white characters.

Many white audiences also praised the movie, although some felt it was biased against them because they misunderstood it as a statement that black people are better than white people. Some black people also found problems with the film and its themes. For example, one of the main antagonists advocates black liberation, just as Garvey and others did. Critics of the film also point out that he is portrayed in a negative, violent way for much of the movie. As professor Kimberlé Crenshaw explained, "Black power has always been framed by its critics as dangerous, irrational, bloodthirsty revenge ... How did that ... trope come to be the central tension in this celebration of Black superheroes?"[1] Just as *The Emperor Jones* raised concerns among some black people and made others excited to see a black actor in a major theatrical production, *Black Panther* created the same mixed feelings in some black audiences.

1. Quoted in Hamid Dabashi, "Watching Black Panther in Harlem," *Al Jazeera*, February 27, 2018, www.aljazeera.com/indepth/opinion/watching-black-panther-harlem-180227091520981.html.

FROM THE SOURCE: PRAISE FOR THE GREEN PASTURES

In his book *Black Manhattan*, James Weldon Johnson highly praised the cast of *The Green Pastures* and its creator Marc Connelly:

[In previous dramas, the] Negro removed any lingering doubts as to his ability to do intelligent acting. In "The Green Pastures," he established conclusively his capacity to get the utmost subtleties across the footlights, to convey the most delicate nuances of emotion, to create the atmosphere in which the seemingly unreal becomes for the audience the most real thing in life. "The Green Pastures" is a play so simple and yet so profound, so close to the earth and yet so spiritual, that it is as high a test for those powers in the actor as any play the American stage has seen—a higher test than many of the immortalized classics ... The acting in "The Green Pastures" seems so spontaneous and natural that one is tempted to believe the players are not really acting. In the light of the truth about the matter, this is a high compliment ... What Mr. Connelly actually did was to work something very little short of a miracle. No one seems able to remember any playwright, play, and company of players that have together received such unanimous praise as these ... in the making of "The Green Pastures."[1]

1. James Weldon Johnson, *Black Manhattan* (New York, NY: Da Capo, 1991), pp. 218–19.

based on Bible stories and biblical figures. Featuring black angels, choirs, and a character called De Lawd (the Lord), Connelly described his work as "an attempt to present certain aspects of a living religion in the terms of its believers. The religion is that of thousands of Negroes in the deep South."[8]

The play was universally praised. With songs performed by the Hall Johnson Choir and Richard B. Harrison playing De Lawd, *The Green Pastures* ran for 557 sold-out performances. The play was then taken on extensive tours in both the North and South before returning to Broadway for a five-year run.

The End of an Era

The Green Pastures was the last great African American drama of the Harlem Renaissance. By the time it debuted, the United States was in the grip of the Great Depression. Many of New York's million-aires lost everything, while more than one-third of American adults were unemployed. In this stressed economy, black Americans were the first to be fired. The trend affected Broadway producers and entertainers as well.

President Franklin D. Roosevelt's federal New Deal program, the Works Progress Administration (WPA), helped a bit by giving grants, or government money, to unemployed artists, writers, and entertainers. Eubie Blake was one of these lucky few; he wrote musicals for the government. Many of Harlem's residents were not so fortunate. The stage lights dimmed, the audiences stayed home—and the Harlem Renaissance faded to black.

How You See History

1. Why do you think *Shuffle Along* was so popular when little notice had been paid to black theater productions in previous years?

2. Why do you think there are so few movies and plays with all-black casts, even today?

3. Do you think views about black theater and movies have changed since the Harlem Renaissance?

CHAPTER FIVE

ART

Theater, literature, and music are all considered art forms, but the term "artist" is most frequently used to describe people who make visual art, such as paintings and sculptures. The visual artists of the Harlem Renaissance were just as active as the playwrights, poets, and musicians.

Sculptor Meta Vaux Warrick Fuller was one artist who, like many of her contemporaries, studied in France for a time to develop her skills and further her career. She moved to Paris in 1899 to study sculpture at the Académie Colarossi and drawing at the École des Beaux-Arts (School of Fine Arts). Although she was only 22 at the time, Fuller's work was admired by French artist Auguste Rodin, whose statue *The Thinker* is one of the most famous sculptures in the world. While in Paris, Fuller also developed a relationship with W. E. B. Du Bois, who encouraged her to explore themes relating to black history and culture in her artwork. In 1903, Fuller entered the prestigious Paris art exhibition known as the Salon d'Automne. The Salon d'Automne, attended by some of the world's most influential artists and art buyers, is known for its famously tough judges. These judges accepted Fuller's masterpiece, *The Wretched*, for the show.

Meta Vaux Warrick Fuller created this sculpture, called *Emancipation*, in 1913 to commemorate the 50th anniversary of the Emancipation Proclamation. In 1999, it was cast in bronze and erected in Harriet Tubman Park in Boston, Massachusetts.

After moving back to the United States, Fuller married a Liberian physician and moved to Framingham, Massachusetts, in 1909. Against the strong disapproval of her husband, Fuller single-handedly built her own sculpture studio. Thanks partially to Du Bois's encouragement, Fuller created the sculpture *Ethiopia Awakening* in 1914. This bronze sculpture symbolizes the emergence of the New Negro from her African roots. Her legs and lower torso are wrapped like a mummy, but a beautiful black woman with long flowing hair and the headdress of an Egyptian queen emerges from the binding.

As a black female artist working during an era of excessive racism and sexism, Fuller keenly understood the concept of breaking free from restraints. She also displayed this theme in the 1919 sculpture *Mary Turner (Silent Protest Against Mob Violence)*. However, unlike *Ethiopia Awakening*, this statue was based on horrific events.

In 1918, a pregnant black woman named Mary Turner was accused of plotting to kill a white man, aided by her husband and two other black men in Valdosta, Georgia. Although the accusations were false, Turner and the three men were lynched, burned, and shot multiple times. In the aftermath, thousands of black people marched in a silent protest down Fifth Avenue in New York City. Fuller was deeply moved by the demonstration and, according to Mary Schmidt Campbell, former executive director of Harlem's Studio Museum, Fuller "memorialized the awakening defiance of her people in her sculpture."[1]

Although Fuller never lived in Harlem, her work inspired Manhattan-based artist Augusta Savage, another female sculptor who struggled against sexism and bigotry.

From an early age, Savage realized that she wanted to become a sculptor, but her Methodist minister father disagreed because he believed art was not Christian. Frustrated that she could not practice her art, Savage moved to New York when she was an adult. When she arrived in Harlem, she worked as a teacher and an artist. Her sculptures reflected black culture and emphasized black facial features. For example, her sculpture *The Harp* was influenced by Negro spirituals and hymns. In 1932, Savage established the

Savage Studio of Arts and Crafts in Harlem to teach adults about art. Five years later, she became the first director of the Harlem Community Art Center, an institution funded by the WPA where black people could learn about their culture through the study of fine arts.

The Paintings of Aaron Douglas

Like Fuller, painter Aaron Douglas worked with a European artist and was strongly influenced by the design elements of African art and African American imagery. Douglas embarked on a successful painting career after moving from Topeka, Kansas, to Harlem in 1925, when he was 26 years old. In New York, his drawings greatly impressed German painter and designer Winold Reiss, who gave Douglas a full scholarship to his art school. Reiss encouraged Douglas to turn away from the European art traditions he learned in school and urged him to express his racial experience through his art, as Du Bois had encouraged Fuller. Douglas did so, exploring issues of race, slavery, and the role of black Americans in the modern world.

Douglas's work cleverly combined several art styles that were extremely popular. He drew on the influences of art deco—a style characterized by geometric forms, sweeping curves, and models with elongated torsos. Many of Douglas's angular, stylized figures are presented as silhouettes. The figures are painted with bodies forward but faces in profile. However, the single eye is drawn as if viewed from the front, not the side. This style is also seen in ancient Egyptian art.

Shortly after his arrival in Harlem, Douglas met Du Bois, who hired him to work in the mailroom at *The Crisis*. Within weeks, however, Douglas was drawing illustrations for articles in the NAACP newspaper. After seeing the quality of his work, Alain Locke commissioned Douglas to create illustrations for *The New Negro*, a book that played a central role in the Harlem Renaissance. Soon after, Charles S. Johnson, who had originally encouraged Douglas to move to New York, began using the artist's work in *Opportunity*.

FROM THE SOURCE: AARON DOUGLAS ON HIS ART STYLE

Aaron Douglas was also inspired by cubism and the art nouveau genre, which used elements found in nature, such as vines, leaves, flowers, birds, and the human form. Describing his style, Douglas stated:

> I wanted to create something new and modern that fitted in with Art Deco and the other things that were taking the country by storm. That is how I came upon the notion to use a number of things such as Cubism and a style with straight lines to emphasize the mathematical relationship of things.[1]

1. Quoted in David Driskell, "The Flowering of the Harlem Renaissance: The Art of Aaron Douglas, Meta Warrick Fuller, Palmer Hayden, and William H. Johnson," in Charles Miers, ed., *Harlem Renaissance: Art of Black America* (New York, NY: Abrams, 1994), p. 110.

With so many famous and respected men as mentors and patrons, Douglas quickly recognized that he was about to become a major success. Like Harlem's literati, he scorned white society and believed black people should use their art to show who they were, regardless of whether it made white people uncomfortable. He moved in with Zora Neale Hurston, Wallace Thurman, and other Harlem bohemians. He also became friends with Langston Hughes and began illustrating his poems in the pages of *Fire!!*. Later, Douglas moved out of the shared house and rented his own apartment, which became a center of social activity for the writers, artists, dancers, musicians, poets, and playwrights of the New Negro movement.

Despite his lively social life, Douglas worked tirelessly to create permanent images during the Harlem Renaissance. In

Like other artists of the Harlem Renaissance, Aaron Douglas used his work to explore racial themes that had previously been ignored.

addition to his newspaper and magazine work, he illustrated book covers for James Weldon Johnson's *The Autobiography of an Ex-Colored Man*, Thurman's *The Blacker the Berry*, and Claude McKay's *Home to Harlem*. These designs feature Douglas's unique flat, silhouetted figures, the lines drawn in such a way as to give a sense of movement to the characters.

The sharp contrasting colors of Douglas's book cover illustrations were softened considerably in a series of paintings that he created at the request of James Weldon Johnson for his book of poems, *God's Trombones: Seven Negro Sermons in Verse*. The book was inspired by Bible stories, black spirituals, recent black history, and black American culture. The paintings, including *Noah's Ark*, *Study for God's Trombones*, and *The Crucifixion*, are executed in various shades of a single color. For example,

Shown here is a cover Aaron Douglas created for a 1926 issue of *Fire!!*

Study for God's Trombones, which depicts a silhouette of a black man standing among jungle plants and struggling with chains, is created in tones of light and dark blue. *The Crucifixion*, with a black man struggling under the weight of a giant cross, is done in various tones of purple. Painted in the style of cubism and the forms of African sculpture, these images showed Douglas as a pioneering artist who invented his own painting genre.

THEY MADE HISTORY: JAMES VAN DER ZEE

Some of the people of the Harlem Renaissance captured the period on film instead of canvas. James Van Der Zee was a photographer who depicted black people in poses showing self-respect, style, and optimism.

Couple Wearing Raccoon Coats is one of Van Der Zee's most famous pictures, and one that encapsulates the era. The picture of a man and a woman posed with their expensive automobile presented a picture of black upper-class life rarely seen in the United States at that time. This was among many of Van Der Zee's photographs showing black people in pursuit of the American Dream at sporting events, family gatherings, weddings, and barbershops. Van Der Zee photographed black celebrities such as Marcus Garvey, heavyweight champion Jack Johnson, dancer Bill "Bojangles" Robinson, and singers Florence Mills and Mamie Smith. Working out of his studio, Guarantee Photos, on 135th Street, Van Der Zee also shot portraits of families, babies, brides, and grooms. His signature technique involved using darkroom tricks and double exposures to give his portraits an interesting edge. For example, *Wedding Portrait with the Superimposed Image of a Little Girl* shows a shadowy youngster holding a doll at the feet of the bride and groom, symbolizing the predicted future of the couple.

Van Der Zee was also a dedicated musician, playing the piano with such jazz giants as Fletcher Henderson. However, he will always be remembered for his photographs that preserve the dignity, independence, and joy of the Harlem residents during the renaissance.

Public Paintings

The paintings for *God's Trombones* sparked an increased demand for Douglas's work. He continued to illustrate for publications, but in 1927, he also painted a mural for the new Club Ebony in Harlem. It was his first large-scale public work. Unveiled when the club opened, the mural was filled with Pan-African cultural symbols in contrast with nature and the modern world.

The mural was a visual history of black music, and some of the dancers and musicians painted beneath the skyscrapers were depictions of real people who were in attendance on opening night. Florence Mills, just back from a whirlwind European tour, was the guest of honor. Other stars included Mac Rae and his Ten Ebony Stompers, Ethel Waters, Paul Robeson, W. E. B. Du Bois, and Wallace Thurman.

The 1929 stock market crash put an end to such glittering Harlem scenes. However, while many of Harlem's performers, artists, and authors struggled, Douglas produced seven murals in seven years, from 1930 to 1937. Critics consider these public paintings to be among the artist's best. Some might never have been painted if not for the Great Depression.

Throughout the 1930s, President Roosevelt's New Deal programs provided WPA art grants to public institutions such as libraries and historically black colleges and universities. One such grant paid for Douglas's *Aspects of Negro Life*.

Douglas also painted murals at Fisk University in Nashville, Tennessee, where he took a job as assistant professor of art education in 1938. He taught painting at Fisk until his retirement in 1966, and he died in Nashville in 1979.

The Harmon Foundation

Many black artists created art based on black American life, culture, legend, and tradition. A number of these artists were introduced to the public through exhibits sponsored by the Harmon Foundation. This prestigious organization, named for white patron of the arts William E. Harmon, began awarding prizes for achievement in art in 1926.

Harmon Foundation exhibitions were seen all over New York City, and these shows provided black artists with widespread exposure to the general public. The publicity attracted black artists from across the country, and the number of artists in the foundation registry grew from about 10 in 1926 to more than 300 in 1929.

Palmer Hayden worked as a custodian to pay for art supplies. He won a Harmon Foundation Gold Award for Distinguished Achievement in Fine Arts in 1926 with the painting *Fétiche et Fleures* (in English, "fetish and flowers"). This work is a still life of an African mask, or fetish, from Gabon; a tablecloth from the Congo; and a table with a vase of flowers. Like other painters at the time, Hayden used African symbols to explore the roots of black American art.

Hayden's contributions to the Harlem Renaissance included depictions of African subjects in their homes, scenes from black folk stories, life in the rural South, and life in Harlem. Hayden had grown up in Wide Water, Virginia, and his childhood memories of small-town residents influenced many of his paintings.

Hayden generated great controversy with his images portraying black people with cartoonish, exaggerated features and grins reminiscent of blackface minstrel shows. His subjects, such as those in *Nous Quatre à Paris* (*We Four in Paris*), often had round, bald heads and large eyes, noses, ears, and lips. Art historian James A. Porter considered these paintings tasteless and said Hayden's work pandered to racist appetites for stereotypical images of black people. Hayden explained that, in his view, black people sometimes acted like minstrel clowns, wearing expressions such as those in his paintings to hide their true feelings when in the presence of white people.

In 1932, Hayden was signed to a WPA program for the US Treasury Art Project. His assignment was to paint scenes of daily life in Harlem. One of the most enduring images from this series is 1938's *Midsummer Night in Harlem*, which shows dozens of figures sitting on stoops in front of Harlem row houses, leaning out apartment windows, or driving in cars. The dark faces

and bright white teeth of the characters offended Porter, who said the painting reminded him of old-time posters for minstrel shows that used to be plastered on city buildings and fences. However, Hayden considered the work satire, saying the humorous and ironic depictions were meant to mock the stereotypes about black people that white people believed. This was based on Du Bois's double-consciousness philosophy, which said black Americans were continually forced to look at themselves through the eyes of their oppressors.

Hayden's most renowned work is from the decades after the Harlem Renaissance. It consists of a series of paintings, created between 1944 and 1954, about the folk hero John Henry. Henry was said to have been a steel-driving man whose ability to lay track for railroads was legendary. He entered into a competition with a steam-powered drill, trying to drive in more spikes and beat the machine. Henry died with his hammer in his hand after winning the contest, so legend says.

Hayden immortalized John

Henry's story on 12 canvases. Commenting on the series, he said that Henry was "a powerful and popular working man who belonged to my section of the country and to my own race."[2] The critically acclaimed series helped Hayden achieve widespread respect, and in later years his work was displayed at prestigious galleries.

William H. Johnson: A Controversial Artist

Like Hayden, artist William H. Johnson often attracted controversy. Although he was trained as a traditional academic painter at the National Academy of Design in New York, he painted in the primitive, folk, or naive style. This style is based on deliberately crude images resembling the drawings of children. When a critic asked Johnson why he abandoned his training as a talented academic painter, he replied, "My aim is to express in a natural way what I feel both rhythmically and spiritually, all that has been saved up in my family of primitiveness and tradition."[3]

Johnson used expressionism combined with an almost cartoonlike technique in brightly colored paintings such as *Chain Gang*, *Young Man in a Vest*, *Café*, and *Sis and L'il Sis*. These paintings are commentaries not only on the positive aspects of black life but also on the social troubles faced by black Americans.

Like many other artists of the Harlem Renaissance, Johnson received less attention and adulation than the authors, singers, musicians, and dancers. However, artwork by Johnson, Douglas, Hayden, Savage, and more provide a priceless visual record of the Jazz Age and the Harlem Renaissance.

Not a Magic Solution

The Harlem Renaissance is remembered as a time of great creativity, when black writers, musicians, and artists helped change widespread attitudes about black people. As Langston Hughes described it, "some Harlemites … thought the race problem had at last been solved through Art … They were sure the New Negro would lead a new life from then on in green pastures of tolerance."[4] It was true that black authors during this time period were published more often, and Broadway plays with all-black casts were largely successful. However, there was a naivete in the belief that things would significantly change for the better. Hughes pointed out that the "ordinary Negro hadn't heard of the Negro Renaissance. And if they had it hadn't raised their wages any."[5] With the onset of the Great Depression at the end of 1929, those already low wages fell dramatically.

In 1933, another economic disaster hit when Prohibition was repealed. The white patrons who flocked to Harlem speakeasies to buy bootleg liquor could now obtain legal drinks in their own neighborhoods. While some Harlem speakeasies converted to legitimate bars, many shut their doors, laying off many black waiters, waitresses, busboys, cooks, bartenders, dancers, musicians, managers, and other employees.

By 1935, nearly half of all Harlem residents were unemployed. The high rents in Harlem had not decreased, however, and many single apartments were now occupied by two or three families. Harlem quickly lost its status as a center of culture. The wealthiest black people were able to leave; black writers and literary promoters such as Hughes, James Weldon Johnson, Charles S. Johnson, and Du Bois fled New York City for cities such as Paris.

The bleak economic conditions in Harlem did not stop poor, uneducated black people from migrating from the South, though. Between 1930 and 1935, another 75,000 black migrants entered New York, most of them settling in Harlem. The poverty, hopelessness, and overcrowding created great stress, which was blamed for the full-blown riot that exploded in Harlem on March 19, 1935. It began when police arrested a Puerto Rican boy for stealing a 10-cent pocketknife from a white-owned business. Rumors spread that the boy had been beaten to death by police, causing a riot as people protested. By the next day, 200 stores were damaged, 3 black people were dead, more than 100 were injured, and nearly $2 million worth of property was destroyed. In reality, the Puerto Rican boy had been released by the police before the riot began because the shopkeeper decided not to press charges, but the riot showed how high tensions had risen in Harlem during the 1930s.

Shown here are Harlem residents cleaning up the damage done during the 1935 riot.

An Enduring Legacy

Harlem was largely ignored by the average American throughout the Great Depression and World War II. However, the influence of the Harlem Renaissance remained strong. In the decades that followed, literature from the era inspired best-selling black authors such as Ralph Ellison, Richard Wright, Toni Morrison, Alice Walker, Octavia Butler, and Maya Angelou to explore black American life. The outstanding jazz music of Duke Ellington, Eubie Blake, and others set a standard by which all other jazz music was measured in later years. It also inspired modern musicians such as Herbie Hancock, Miles Davis, and Wynton Marsalis.

Art was not the only influence on following generations; the political aspects of the Harlem Renaissance influenced a new generation of black leaders in the 1950s and 1960s. Nation of Islam leader Malcolm X and civil rights icon Martin Luther King Jr. both credited Marcus Garvey and founders of the New Negro movement for redefining black consciousness, and the progress of the era served as a starting point from which black Americans gained a spirit of self-determination and pride. In the mid-1960s, this was expressed as Black Power and through the expression "Black Is Beautiful." In more recent years, this way of asserting the importance of race and equality has been seen in global movements such as Black Lives Matter and in public figures such as National Football League (NFL) player Colin Kaepernick and the many people he inspired to "take a knee" during the national anthem to protest racism. It is even seen in government, such as when Barack Obama became the first black president of the United States—a position he held for two terms, from 2009 to 2017.

The Harlem Renaissance was short-lived, but it has had a lasting effect on black culture throughout the United States and around the world. Although black people still face racism, the struggles of the Harlem Renaissance artists, playwrights, musicians, and writers helped smooth the path for modern black creators, making today's cultural landscape much more interesting and diverse.

How You See History

1. Why do you think some black artists' work made white people uncomfortable?

2. How do you think being a woman as well as being black affected Fuller's work?

3. What were some of the lasting effects of the Harlem Renaissance?

TIMELINE

1917
Marcus Garvey moves the headquarters of the United Negro Improvement Association (UNIA) to Harlem.

February 17, 1919
The Harlem Hellfighers march in a victory parade upon their return from World War I.

1920
Eugene O'Neill's play *The Emperor Jones* debuts in November; Prohibition begins, causing many speakeasies to open in Harlem.

1921
Shuffle Along opens on Broadway in New York City.

1923
Bessie Smith records "Down Hearted Blues," saving Columbia Records from bankruptcy; the legendary Cotton Club opens in Harlem; James P. Johnson composes "The Charleston."

March 21, 1924
Charles S. Johnson hosts the NUL Civic Club Dinner.

1925
Langston Hughes's first major poem, "The Weary Blues," is published.

1926
Harlem's Savoy Ballroom opens; Zora Neale Hurston collaborates with Wallace Thurman, Richard Nugent, and painter Aaron Douglas on the magazine *Fire!!*.

1927

Duke Ellington and his band are hired to play at the Cotton Club; *Porgy* premieres on Broadway; Aaron Douglas unveils his first large-scale public work for the New Ebony Club in Harlem.

1929

The Great Depression begins.

1932

Huge numbers of black Americans leave New York to travel abroad; sculptor Augusta Savage establishes the Savage Studio of Arts and Crafts in Harlem to teach adults about art.

1935

The Works Progress Administration (WPA) provides government-sponsored jobs to many Harlem-based artists and writers.

NOTES

Introduction: The Revival of a Culture

1. Paul Laurence Dunbar, *The Sport of the Gods* (New York, NY: Dodd, Mead and Company, 1902), pp. 77–78.
2. Cary D. Wintz, *Black Culture and the Harlem Renaissance* (Houston, TX: Rice University Press, 1988), p. 3.

Chapter One: Change in the City

1. Leon Litwack, *Trouble in Mind: Black Southerners in the Age of Jim Crow* (New York, NY: Alfred A. Knopf, 1998), p. xiv.
2. James Weldon Johnson, "Harlem: The Culture Capital," in Alain Locke, ed., *The New Negro* (New York, NY: Touchstone, 1997), pp. 306–07.
3. Johnson, "Harlem: The Culture Capital," in Sondra Kathryn Wilson, ed., *The Selected Writings of James Weldon Johnson, Volume II: Social, Political, and Literary Essays* (New York, NY: Oxford University Press, 1995), p. 385.
4. Quoted in Tim Brooks and Richard Keith Spottswood, *Lost Sounds: Blacks and the Birth of the Recording Industry, 1890–1919* (Chicago, IL: University of Illinois Press, 2004), p. 280.
5. Quoted in Theodore G. Vincent, ed., *Voices of a Black Nation* (Trenton, NJ: Africa World, 1990), p. 96.
6. Quoted in Theodore Kornweibel Jr., *Seeing Red: Federal Campaigns Against Black Militancy, 1919–1925* (Bloomington, IN: Indiana University Press, 1998), p. 102.

Chapter Two: Literature

1. Langston Hughes, *The Fight for Freedom: The Story of the NAACP* (New York, NY: Norton, 1962), p. 203.
2. James Weldon Johnson, *Along This Way: The Autobiography of James Weldon Johnson* (New York, NY: Viking Press, 1933), p. 203.
3. Claude McKay, *Harlem Shadows: The Poems of Claude McKay* (New York, NY: Harcourt, Brace and Company, 1922), p. 53.
4. Quoted in Heather Hathaway, "Exploring 'Something New':

The 'Modernism' of Claude McKay's *Harlem Shadows*," in Hathaway, Josef Jarab, and Jeffrey Melnick, eds., *Race and the Modern Artist* (New York, NY: Oxford University Press, 2003), e-book.

5. James Weldon Johnson, "The Dilemma of the Negro Author," *American Mercury* (December 1928): p. 478.

6. Quoted in David Levering Lewis, *When Harlem Was in Vogue* (New York, NY: Alfred A. Knopf, 1981), p. 124.

7. Langston Hughes, "The Weary Blues," Poetry Foundation, accessed December 6, 2019, www.poetryfoundation.org/poems/47347/the-weary-blues.

8. Langston Hughes, *The Big Sea* (New York, NY: Hill and Wang, 1993), p. 266.

9. Hughes, *The Big Sea*, p. 267.

10. Hughes, *The Big Sea*, p. 235.

11. "The Mission," *FIYAH*, accessed December 6, 2019, www.fiyahlitmag.com/the-mission.

Chapter Three: Music

1. Langston Hughes, *The Big Sea* (New York, NY: Hill and Wang, 1993), pp. 224–25.

2. Quoted in Malgorzata Ziólek-Sowinska, "African American Modernism and the Music of Duke Ellington," in Isabel Soto and Violet Showers Johnson, eds., *Western Fictions, Black Realities: Meanings of Blackness and Modernities* (East Lansing, MI: Michigan State University Press, 2011), p. 215.

3. Cary D. Wintz, *Harlem Speaks: A Living History of the Harlem Renaissance* (Chicago, IL: Sourcebooks, 2007), p. 36.

4. Quoted in Wintz, *Harlem Speaks*, pp. 179–80.

Chapter Four: Theater

1. David Krasner, *A Beautiful Pageant: African American Theatre, Drama, and Performance in the Harlem Renaissance, 1910–1927* (New York, NY: Palgrave Macmillan, 2003), p. 229.

2. Langston Hughes and Milton Meltzer, *Black Magic: A Pictorial History of the African-American in the Performing Arts* (New York, NY: Perseus Books, 1967), p. 123.

3. James Weldon Johnson, *Black Manhattan* (New York, NY: Da Capo, 1991), p. 170.
4. Allen Woll, *Black Musical Theatre: From Coontown to Dreamgirls* (Baton Rouge, LA: Louisiana State University, 1989), p. 60.
5. Quoted in Krasner, *A Beautiful Pageant*, p. 241.
6. Quoted in Al Rose, *Eubie Blake* (New York, NY: Schirmer, 1979), p. 74.
7. Quoted in Woll, *Black Musical Theatre*, p. 65.
8. Quoted in Johnson, *Black Manhattan*, p. 219.

Chapter Five: Art

1. Mary Schmidt Campbell, "Introduction," in Charles Miers, ed., *Harlem Renaissance: Art of Black America* (New York, NY: Abrams, 1994), p. 27.
2. Quoted in Lara Kuykendall, "Palmer Hayden's John Henry Series: Inventing an American Hero," in Cynthia Fowler, ed., *Locating American Art: Finding Art's Meaning in Museums, Colonial Period to the Present* (New York, NY: Routledge, 2017), e-book.
3. Quoted in Theresa A. Leininger-Miller, *New Negro Artists in Paris* (New Brunswick, NJ: Rutgers University Press, 2001), p. 97.
4. Langston Hughes, *The Big Sea* (New York, NY: Hill and Wang, 1993), p. 228.
5. Hughes, *The Big Sea*, p. 228.

Books: Nonfiction

Arora, Sabina G. *The Great Migration and the Harlem Renaissance.* New York, NY: Britannica Educational Publishing, 2016.

Crompton, Samuel Willard. *Langston Hughes: Jazz Poet of the Harlem Renaissance.* New York, NY: Enslow Publishing, 2020.

Herringshaw, DeAnn. *The Harlem Renaissance.* North Mankato, MN: ABDO Publishing, 2012.

Winter, Jonah, and Keith Mallett. *How Jelly Roll Morton Invented Jazz.* New York, NY: Roaring Brook Press, 2015.

Books: Fiction

Johnson, James Weldon. *The Autobiography of an Ex-Colored Man.* New York, NY: Alfred A. Knopf, 1927.

Hurston, Zora Neale. *Their Eyes Were Watching God.* New York, NY: Harper Perennial, 2006.

Websites

BrainPOP: Harlem Renaissance
www.brainpop.com/socialstudies/africanamericanhistory/harlemrenaissance
This interactive website offers information and activities relating to
the Harlem Renaissance.

Drop Me Off in Harlem
artsedge.kennedy-center.org/interactives/harlem
This website features many of the famous faces of the Harlem
Renaissance, including visual artists, authors, activists, and musicians.

The Harlem Renaissance
historyoftheharlemrenaissance.weebly.com
This website offers information about some of the most influential
people and places of the Harlem Renaissance.

HISTORY: Harlem Renaissance
history.com/topics/black-history/harlem-renaissance
Watch videos and listen to speeches about the Harlem Renaissance
on this website, which also feature short biographies of some of the
era's most celebrated talents.

A New African American Identity: The Harlem Renaissance
nmaahc.si.edu/blog-post/new-african-american-identity-harlem-renaissance
The National Museum of African American History & Culture presents
this overview of the Harlem Renaissance.

ABOUT THE AUTHOR

Meghan Green has edited a number of books for young people on the topics of social justice and self-esteem. She also sometimes gives talks at local schools on these topics. She is a social worker who specializes in working with developmentally disabled individuals. Meghan lives in Pennsylvania with her husband, Kris.